MAK...
MAK...

BY
DAPHNE CLAIR

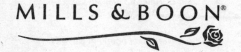

MILLS & BOON®

*First published in Great Britain 1999
Harlequin Mills & Boon Limited,
Eton House, 18-24 Paradise Road, Richmond, Surrey TW9 1SR*

© Daphne Clair de Jong 1999

ISBN 0 263 81667 2

*Set in Times Roman 10½ on 12 pt.
01-9905-46763 C1*

*Printed and bound in Norway
by AIT Trondheim AS, Trondheim*

CHAPTER ONE

'BUT what about the wedding?' Stefanie Varney's mother wailed, looking up from the flimsy single page she had just read. A perfect pink carnation slipped from the fingers of her other hand, the big vases of mixed blooms forgotten behind her. 'Everything's been arranged for tomorrow!'

The utility room was strewn with roses, carnations, chrysanthemums and ferns, the perfume of the flowers cloying in the small space. They were supposed to have been placed in the church tonight.

'There isn't going to be a wedding.' Stefanie distractedly brushed back a strand of fine, dark brown hair that had strayed across her eyes. 'At least, not for me.'

She was surprised that her voice sounded normal, if a bit flat. When she'd come home early from work and taken the several letters waiting for her to her room, she'd opened Bryan's first, touched and pleased that he'd bothered to write to her when this evening he'd be driving down from Auckland for their wedding rehearsal, bringing her chief bridesmaid with him.

Once she'd read the letter and absorbed its contents her instinct had been to hide it away—hide herself too, stay in her room and pretend this wasn't happening. Because it couldn't be.

'It wouldn't be so bad,' Patti said, 'if he'd said something earlier! Oh, this is *awful*!' Then, as if realising what it meant for her daughter, she stepped forward and enfolded Stefanie in a maternal embrace. 'My poor darling—I'm so sorry!'

With her mother's tears wetting her cheek Stefanie returned the hug, while her own eyes remained stubbornly dry. Everything seemed unreal.

But she wasn't the only one affected. More than a hundred people had been invited to attend the wedding. More than a hundred friends and relatives—both hers and Bryan's.

Patti was sobbing now. Gently Stefanie freed herself. 'I'm all right,' she said. 'But we have to let people know.'

'Yes, but there's so little time! The caterers...the guests...the church! What on earth are we going to say to everyone?'

'That the wedding will not now take place?' Stefanie offered. 'I think that's the usual form.'

'How can you be so calm,' her mother marvelled almost crossly, fishing for a handkerchief, 'when you've just been left practically at the altar?'

Inwardly Stefanie winced. At least Bryan had spared her that, if only by a hair's breadth. 'We weren't exactly at the altar.'

'As near as makes no difference!' Patti said viciously. 'How *could* he? And Noelle? Your chief bridesmaid! She's supposed to be your best friend! I always knew there was something about that girl!'

There was—something that Bryan, like so many other men, had evidently found irresistible.

Something that Stefanie had never envied until now—a kind of vulnerable, lush yet innocent sexuality that Stefanie knew she would never have had, even if like Noelle she'd been a petite, curvy blonde with big violet-blue eyes instead of being averagely tall, average-looking, her eyes an indeterminate grey-blue flecked with amber. As a tall, gangly teenager she'd wondered if she would ever develop a bust, and even now it was nothing spectacular. Although Noelle professed to envy her friend's long legs, Stefanie had never been the object of the kind of instant male attention that Noelle attracted.

Foolishly, she'd thought Bryan was immune, perhaps by dint of having grown up in the same town as both her and Noelle. But he wouldn't have seen much of Noelle between her leaving with her family to live in New Zealand's largest city, and meeting her again at his and Stefanie's engagement party, shortly before Noelle had announced her own engagement. Presumably he'd viewed her since then through new eyes.

Something seemed to be squeezing Stefanie's heart into a small, cold ball. Bryan and Noelle. Coupling the names in her mind, she felt a bleak sense of dislocation. This was going to hurt like hell when the unnatural detachment wore off, but right now she could almost believe it was all happening to someone else while she looked on, a distant observer.

And she was grateful for the illusion. There were things to think about, things that must be done before tomorrow. She said, 'I wonder if Quinn knows.'

'Noelle's fiancé? Do you think she's told him?'

'I hope so.' Although Stefanie was doubtful. She didn't know Quinn Branson very well, but even at their first meeting she had gained a definite impression of smouldering masculine power.

They'd attended a function in Auckland as a foursome—Noelle's idea. Noelle and Stefanie were briefly alone while the men got drinks, and as they'd waited another man approached, hopefully ogling Noelle. Quinn, swiftly returning to her side, had warned the interloper off with no more than a look.

Noelle hadn't seemed to mind, snuggling up to Quinn, raising her adoring gaze to his stern face and making it relax into a smile, indulgent but subtly laced with desire. Stefanie remembered that look vividly.

Her guess was that he wouldn't have tamely accepted the news that Noelle was leaving him for someone else. And Noelle had never stood up well to angry confrontations. More likely she had followed Bryan's example and sent him a Dear John letter.

Patti started to cry again. 'Oh, how *could* they?' Her voice rose. 'Do you suppose Bryan's parents know? They would have been in touch, surely! What's your father going to say? And Tracey was *so* looking forward to being a bridesmaid.'

Like her mother, seventeen-year-old Tracey burst into tears when she was told the news. Gwenda, the middle and married one of the Varneys' three daughters, having rushed to the house in response to an incoherent call from Patti, sharply advised her younger sibling to stop being such a baby and think how poor Stefanie must feel.

Gwenda had always been the practical one. It was she who broke the news to their father when he arrived and found them all sitting around the table in the big kitchen-cum-dining room, while Stefanie stared into the dregs of the well-sweetened coffee Gwenda had almost forced her to drink.

Stephen Varney's first explosive words of shocked fury made Patti wince. But even she didn't protest, perhaps glad that someone in the family was giving vent to what they were all feeling.

His gaze on Stefanie's pale face, he said, 'Are you all right, Stef?'

'Yes.' She tried to smile, but her lips felt as if they were made of tyre rubber.

'If it will help,' he offered, 'I'll tear the young bastard limb from limb.'

Stefanie stifled a forlorn laugh. The idea of her scholarly and gentle schoolteacher father doing violence to her erstwhile bridegroom was ludicrous, although she appreciated the thought. 'Thank you, Dad, but I don't see that it would do any good.'

'It might make me feel better,' he told her grimly. 'But if he still means something to you...' His eyes questioned her anxiously.

'Right now I don't know what I feel,' Stefanie confessed. 'I've known Bryan practically all my life. I can't suddenly change my feelings just like that.'

'He wasn't good enough for you.' Her father came over to her and squeezed her shoulder. 'Bryan always seemed a bit lightweight to me.'

He didn't mean physically, of course. Bryan was solidly built and an accomplished sportsman. He had narrowly missed selection as an All Black, representing New Zealand on the rugby fields of the world. That was when Stefanie had seen a new side of him, a vulnerable, unsure side that aroused her compassion and, eventually, her love.

Her left hand felt oddly empty and weightless. Bryan's letter had told her to keep his ring, but she could never wear it again, not even as a dress ring. She'd removed the gold circlet with its cluster of little diamonds from her finger and carefully placed it on her dressing table before she went to break the news to her mother.

'There isn't enough time to write to people,' Patti fretted. 'We'll have to phone everyone tonight. And some of them are already travelling.'

'Where's the guest list?' Gwenda asked. 'We'd better start going through it. Bryan's people can get in touch with everyone from their side—Mum, you'd better phone them and make sure he *has* told them. Have you contacted the minister? Daddy, you look after Stefanie.'

Over her feeble protest, Stephen steered Stefanie out into the hallway, closing the door behind them. 'Your mother and your sisters and I will see the arrangements are cancelled. You don't need to be involved.'

'But Gwenda's pregnant—should she…?'

'Gwenda's fine. She's got over the queasy stage, and you know how she loves to organise. I'll keep an eye on her.'

The front doorbell rang imperatively, and Stephen dropped his arm from her, going to answer it.

Maybe when she was alone again she'd be able to cry, to let her feelings out of their tight imprisonment.

Already retreating to her room along the broad old-fashioned passageway, Stefanie heard her father say in tones of surprise, 'Quinn, isn't it? What can I do for you?'

A deep, faintly familiar male voice answered, 'I'd like to see your daughter, Mr Varney. Please. Stefanie?'

'I'm afraid Stefanie isn't available right now,' Stephen said. 'It might be better if you called at another time—'

'You know what's happened?' Quinn Branson enquired roughly. '*She* does?'

'Yes, we know. So you'll understand…'

A pause. 'I realise she's probably extremely upset. Would you tell her I'd like to talk to her?'

'I really don't think—'

Stefanie turned, went back down the passageway and touched her father's arm. 'It's all right.' Presumably Quinn was shocked and upset too. She wasn't sure what good it would do, but if he was so desperate to speak to her she could at least give him a few minutes of her time. It wasn't as though there was much else to do with the rest of her disastrous day. 'Why don't you come in?' she invited the tall, dark-suited man standing on the doorstep.

His expression changing from tight-lipped grimness to slight puzzlement as he studied her determinedly calm face and tearless eyes, he nodded curtly in greeting.

'This way,' she said. 'We'll be in the sitting room, Dad.'

Her father cast her a measuring look, then reluctantly moved aside as Quinn accepted the invitation and stepped through the doorway, for a moment appearing to fill it. She hadn't remembered his shoulders were so broad, but they didn't seem out of proportion to his slimmer waist and hips and long, immaculately trousered legs.

'Come in here.' Stefanie led the visitor into the big, comfortable front room and closed the door. 'Please sit down.'

Quinn glanced at the fat floral sofa and matching chairs. 'Thanks, but I'm not staying. And I've been sitting long enough in the car.'

'You've just driven from Auckland?'

'It's only an hour and a half. I would have been driving down tomorrow anyway.'

As her bridesmaid's fiancé he'd had an invitation. Bryan was supposed to have been bringing Noelle with him tonight for the rehearsal.

He stood on the cream carpet and looked at her with a raking gaze. The few times they had met, she had never noticed that his eyes were so deep a green—like dark, polished Southland jade, fathomless and yet hard.

'How are you?' he asked abruptly.

'Fine,' she answered, meeting the conventional query with a conventional reply. 'Are you sure you won't sit—?'

'No, I mean how are you really?' he interrupted. 'I was afraid I'd find you in hysterical tears. Or still in blissful ignorance of what's going on.'

Stefanie hesitated. 'I don't think I've ever been hysterical. How are *you*?'

'Bloody furious,' he answered. 'Aren't you?'

He *was* furious, she realised now, despite his calm demeanour. It was in the way he held himself, rigidly controlled, and in the line carved between his black brows under hair nearly as dark. Even, maybe, in the intense sheen of his eyes. And certainly in the harshness of his tone.

'I suppose I'm in shock,' she said candidly. 'Sort of numb.'

He inspected her narrowly then. 'Are you going to be okay? Will your family look after you?'

'Oh, yes. Too well, probably. I'll be an object of sympathy for months,' Stefanie guessed, inwardly shuddering. 'Maybe years.' And if she never married after all, possibly for ever. 'It's going to be hell. Sorry, I don't mean to cry on your shoulder.'

'You're not crying,' he pointed out. Again that rather disconcerting stare was levelled at her. 'You don't even look as though you *have* cried.'

He sounded almost accusing. In similar circumstances Noelle would have been in floods of tears.

'Maybe I will later when it sinks in. What did you want?'

'Will you?' he queried, ignoring her question. The slightest elevation of the straight, thick brows seemed to doubt it. 'You're remarkably composed for a jilted bride.'

The tiny tremor that ran through her must have shown on her face. Surprisingly, Quinn's cheeks darkened. 'That was crass,' he apologised. 'My only excuse is I've been caught off guard—as I suppose you have.' The probing gaze made it a question.

'If I'd had any idea,' Stefanie assured him, 'I would have freed Bryan immediately.'

'To run off with my fiancée?' Quinn enquired with a flash of bitter irony. 'Very self-sacrificing of you.'

'Not at all,' Stefanie retorted. 'I wouldn't want to be married to a man who's in love with someone else. Would you?'

A flicker of savage humour momentarily lit his face. 'I wasn't planning to marry a man.'

'You know what I mean!'

'Sorry. Not the right time for stupid wisecracks. Do you have any idea where they've gone?'

Surely he didn't have some crazy notion that he could drag *his fiancée* as he'd called her so possessively, back to his side? 'You're not thinking of following them, are you? I know you're angry, but what good would it do to—well…whatever you're thinking of doing?'

'Are you worried about your—about Bryan? I'd have thought you'd be grateful if I knocked his teeth down his throat.'

What was it with men? Even her father had offered to tear Bryan limb from limb. 'I don't believe violence solves anything.'

'As a matter of fact I agree with you—in most circumstances,' Quinn said. 'If I promised not to spoil Bryan's pretty face would you tell me where you think they are?'

'What about Noelle's pretty face?'

His grim expression changed to angry shock. 'I've never hit a woman in my life! I swear I never would!'

'Anyway,' Stefanie said, 'I have no idea.'

He cocked his head. 'You couldn't make an educated guess?'

'We—Bryan and I—had booked a flight to Australia and a hotel near the Great Barrier Reef for our…our honeymoon.' With a certain irony of her own, she added, 'Maybe he's taken Noelle there instead.'

Quinn gave a caustic crack of laughter, quickly suppressed. 'You're not serious!'

'No,' Stefanie conceded. 'But then, what do I know about Bryan—after fifteen years?' She would never have expected him to do this to her.

'You've known him that long?' His frowning gaze turned curious.

'Since we were kids. Ratanui's not a big town— we were in the same class at primary school, and then at high school.'

Boy-like, Bryan had scarcely deigned to notice her

until they were both going on fourteen, when during a neighbourhood barbecue in the Varneys' yard he'd clumsily kissed her in the darkness under the old magnolia tree.

Years later they'd laughed about that—the first kiss for both of them, and not at all successful. After they became engaged he teased her that he'd had to find other girls to practise with before daring to approach her again. She knew there had been plenty of them. But she had been sure she'd be the last. So much for certainty.

'Were you in love with him?'

She met Quinn's concentrated stare. 'Of course. We were getting married.'

'Tomorrow.'

'Yes.'

'It must be a hell of a shock for you. At least our wedding—Noelle's and mine—was weeks away.' The frown line deepened. He looked away from her, seemingly lost in thought, but perhaps trying to hide emotions that he didn't want her to see.

Noelle's invitations had already gone out. Had she left Quinn to deal with that too? 'I suppose we'll get over it,' Stefanie suggested hopefully, although at the moment it was hard to imagine. Her heart felt peculiarly hollow. 'For myself, I'm damned if I'm going to let this ruin my life.'

His gaze returned to her with a hint of respect. 'It could ruin mine,' he said. 'Or at least my business.'

'Your business?' She recalled Noelle had said he'd set up his own computer consultancy about a year ago.

He shook his head. 'Never mind. I needn't burden

you with my problems. You have enough of your own. If there's anything I can do to help...?'

An offer that he probably didn't expect her to take him up on, but it was nice of him to make it. 'Thanks,' Stefanie said, 'but you have your own problems too.'

'Yes. Damn it, I do.' He moved restlessly, the frown becoming a scowl of temper. 'I thought Noelle loved me. Wanted to be with me.'

Stefanie bit her tongue. It was hardly the moment to tell Quinn that this wasn't the first time Noelle had thought she loved someone and then changed her mind. She'd never got as far as an engagement before. Stefanie too had hoped that this time her friend was sure of her feelings. 'I'm sorry,' she said.

His glance at her was almost impatient. '*You* don't need to apologise.'

'It was an expression of sympathy, not an apology.'

He grunted. 'Thanks, but it's unnecessary. When did you find out? And how? Did Bryan have the guts to face you with it?' His scornful tone expressed his scepticism.

'He wrote me a letter. I got it this afternoon when I came home.'

'Bastard,' Quinn said unemotionally.

'How did Noelle break the news to you?' she asked.

'A message on my answer-machine. At the office. She knew I was out of the country and wouldn't hear it until I got back today.'

'Bitch.' Stefanie echoed his tone.

He laughed shortly. 'Thanks for that.'

'So why do you want to find her? Are you hoping to persuade her to come back to you?'

He didn't answer immediately. Perhaps he hadn't thought it through. 'No,' he said finally, 'I don't want her back. Not in the way you mean.'

Stefanie blinked, puzzled, and he said, 'I suppose I did hope she might change her mind—again—if I confronted her. That she's just trying to teach me a lesson, expecting I'll chase after her and tell her I can't live without her. On second thoughts I don't think I'll give her that satisfaction.'

He sounded quite ruthless, as if he could cut Noelle out of his life without a pang. But Stefanie didn't think he was a man who easily showed his feelings, and maybe underneath the inflexible exterior he was smarting. 'A lesson?' she enquired.

'It doesn't matter. You don't want to hear all about our lovers' spat.'

'You had a quarrel?'

'I didn't think she meant it.' He was staring at the carpet.

'Meant what?'

'That if I kept on with this project I was pursuing overseas she might not be here when I came back.' His head lifted.

'You didn't listen to her?' Stefanie guessed.

Quinn was watching her thoughtfully. 'Do I detect a hint of female solidarity, even after what she's done to you?'

'You mean, taken my man?' Stefanie returned his look. 'She couldn't have if he hadn't wanted to be taken. It was Bryan's own decision.'

Quinn gave a reluctant nod. 'I see your point. And I guess that's sauce for the gander too.' He paused. 'Are they planning to marry, do you know?'

'Bryan just wrote that they wanted to be together.

He didn't say they were leaving Auckland, but he's got three weeks' holiday...' For what was supposed to have been their honeymoon.

'And Noelle said they were going away together, whatever that means. I guess she didn't want to be around when I came home and found her message. Even though I caught an earlier connection in Nandi than I expected, they'd already left.'

He must be wondering if it would have made a difference if he'd been in time to see Noelle, and try to stop her. Stefanie felt a pang of sympathy.

Quinn thrust a hand into his pocket. 'I hope they're enjoying themselves.'

Of course he didn't, Stefanie knew. He was still angry and no doubt frustrated, with no one to vent his reined-in temper on. Maybe that was really why he'd wanted to pursue Noelle—to tell her and Bryan what he thought of their actions.

It crossed Stefanie's mind that in a way she couldn't blame Noelle for ducking the issue, making sure she was well away before Quinn got a chance to challenge her decision. He wasn't as obviously muscular as Bryan, but he must be a couple of inches taller and his body language spoke of coiled whipcord strength. Not to mention the masterful jaw and a nose that brought Roman emperors vaguely to mind.

The man had a formidable presence that had nothing to do with physical threat. In relaxed social situations that potent masculinity had been less overt, but there was no mistaking it today.

Maybe if Noelle had dared to face him with her sudden change of heart he'd have talked her out of it. Stefanie believed his vehement claim that he'd never hit a woman, but there were other forms of persuasion—even of coercion. Instinct and his blunt insistence on seeing her today told her that Quinn wasn't a man who easily took no for an answer. Maybe that was how he'd got Noelle to wear his ring in the first place. Although she'd seemed happily excited and proud when she'd first shown it to her friends. 'I'm afraid I can't help you,' Stefanie said. 'I really have no idea where they might be hi—I mean, where they might be.'

He cocked his head, his eyes narrowing. 'Why do I get the feeling you wouldn't tell me if you did?'

Had he read her mind? 'I don't know,' she said. 'That's academic, isn't it, since I can't anyway?'

'Hmm.' But if he still doubted her word he didn't press her.

'You could have phoned,' Stefanie suggested, 'instead of driving all this way.'

'I did, earlier. Your mother obviously had no idea what was going on, and I had a nasty feeling that Bryan was going to let you turn up at the church tomorrow and find out then.'

The thought made her feel sicker than she did already. 'Bryan would never have done that to me.' But her certainty wavered at Quinn's silently lifted brows.

Her mother hadn't mentioned a call from Quinn— with all the drama Patti must have totally forgotten about it. 'You…said nothing to my mother?'

'No.' His eyes darkened. 'Maybe I was wrong, but I figured if I were you I'd rather hear it face to face, not as a passed-on telephone message from a virtual stranger. And if Bryan wasn't going to do it, then as the other person directly involved in this mess it seemed to be down to me.'

In the midst of his own pain and anger he'd taken

the time to drive from Auckland to Ratanui to break the news to her in person. 'That was thoughtful of you,' she said. 'I'm sorry you came all this way for nothing.'

'I needed to do something anyway.' He rocked on his heels, hands thrust into his pockets. 'It was the only active thing I could think of that was even marginally useful...to anyone. And now I've taken up enough of your time. Thanks for seeing me.' That penetrating gaze swiftly encompassed her again. 'I'm glad to see you're bearing up so well.'

'So are you.'

She thought he almost smiled, or perhaps he only tried to. 'Perhaps we'll meet again—in more... pleasant circumstances.'

'I hope so,' Stefanie agreed politely. She wasn't sure she'd want to meet him again. Probably he felt the same, despite his courteous words. No one wanted to be reminded of hurt and humiliation. If they did cross paths, this ghastly day would be the first thing that would come to their minds.

It was a day that both of them surely wanted to forget.

CHAPTER TWO

WHEN she did see him again, less than a month later, Stefanie experienced an odd sense of fatalism.

She was sitting alone in a crowded café in the middle of Wellington, dispiritedly pulling apart a piece of gooey cake that she'd decided had been a mistake.

Sensing the man with a tray in his hands pausing beside her, she looked up and wasn't even surprised to find Quinn Branson's steady dark green gaze surveying her.

'Hello, Stefanie,' he said, adding after a small pause, 'May I...?'

He would have had to ask to share her table now that she'd seen him, even if the café hadn't been almost full. And she had no choice but to nod her permission for him to take the empty chair opposite, and try to give him a smile of welcome.

'What are you doing here?' Quinn enquired, tearing open a packet of sugar.

Running away, she might have told him. She'd fled to the capital after her aborted wedding precisely so that she could lose herself in a large city far from both Ratanui and Auckland, and considerably lessen the chances of bumping into anyone who knew her. The head librarian had been very understanding of her desire to find another job—any job outside her home town. 'But don't burn your boats,' she'd advised. 'I appreciate your letting me know your plans, but you have three weeks' leave anyway, and if you want to come back after all we'll be happy to have you.'

It was just one of many kindnesses by many people. Knowing she ought to be grateful, Stefanie was instead heartily relieved to be away from the sympathy and the curiosity of the good people of Ratanui. But she'd already been in Wellington more than two weeks, and was getting a little desperate.

Given the way her day had gone so far, it was only to be expected that she'd choose the same café for her long-delayed lunch as the very last person she ever wanted to see again—with the possible exception of her ex-fiancé or her erstwhile best friend. 'I'm looking for a job,' she said.

Stirring the sugar into his coffee, Quinn nodded silently. 'Any luck?'

'Not a lot. I was on a short list until today, but I've just found out someone else got the position. There's a lot of competition for jobs in Wellington.'

'You're a qualified librarian, aren't you?'

'Yes.' She'd been the First Assistant and in line to take over the top job in the Ratanui Library when the present head retired. 'But I'd take just about anything.' Anything that would put food in her mouth and a roof over her head, that would keep her away from the small town where practically everyone knew what had happened to her. 'Only I've no experience of any other work except a bit of fruit-picking.'

'Have you ever lived away from home before?' Quinn asked.

'I stayed in a hostel here in Wellington when I went to Library School.'

'How did you like it?'

'The bookshops and the Arts Festival and the concerts were great, but I'm not really a city person. I was lucky there was a job for me in Ratanui.'

'You enjoy library work?'

'I like being around books, and finding what people want, whether it's a good read or a piece of information. Tracking down research material for someone gives me a buzz. Just about everyone in town comes into the library sooner or later, even if they don't visit it regularly.'

His hand curving about his coffee cup, Quinn looked down at it. 'I guess that could be a problem for you right now.'

'Yes,' Stefanie agreed simply. 'It's a very public sort of job. If I have to go back to Ratanui after all I'm going to be an object of pity for the whole town.'

He looked up, and she thought irrelevantly what striking eyes he had. They looked less jade-like today, less green and hard, with a softer light in them. 'Sounds rough. Your family is supportive, though? You said they'd look after you.'

Stefanie laughed ruefully. 'My mother kept crying and asking me if I was all right, my younger sister spent most of her time assuring me I was better off without Bryan, and telling everyone what a rotten creep he turned out to be. My mother's friends brought over baking and flowers for me as if someone had died, and every time I put a foot outside the door the neighbours asked me how I was feeling, dear. And my friends didn't know what to say. Whenever someone casually mentioned the words ''engagement'' or ''wedding'' there was an embarrassed sort of hush while they all waited for me to burst into tears.'

Quinn regarded her with a sort of dispassionate sympathy. 'No wonder you want to get out of there.'

The sympathy was almost unnerving. A lump constricted Stefanie's throat as she gazed into Quinn's fathomless eyes, and saw them darken as he gazed back at her. She had a fleeting urge to throw herself on his broad male chest and feel the strength of his arms about her.

Mentally she shook herself, looking away. She'd come to Wellington precisely to escape sympathy and willing shoulders to cry on. 'How are you getting on?' she asked him. 'Is everyone smothering you with pity too?'

'They know I wouldn't welcome it. I saw my parents and told them the wedding's off. They'll tell anyone else who needs to know. With a bit of luck and some fast talking I'll be leaving the country soon anyway, and by the time I get back it'll be old news.'

'Lucky you.'

'Maybe.'

Meaning he'd lost his fiancée, and like herself he had a bruised and aching heart. Stefanie bit her lip. 'Where are you going?'

'Busiata, for at least six months. Provided it comes off after all.' A line deepened between his dark brows. 'I'm here to finalise the contract with the consul.'

'What on earth are you going to do for that long on a dot in the middle of the Pacific?'

Faint amusement lit his eyes. 'It may be a dot on the map, but it's actually quite a substantial little island, with a population of over eight thousand.'

'Still—what's a computer consultant going to do there? They don't even have a tourist industry, do they? Just a tiny export business in coconuts and bananas?'

'That's the whole point.' He picked up a sandwich.

'King Suniasisi wants me to help bring the place into the twenty-first century by setting up a computer centre and offering worldwide services via satellite.'

Stefanie stared. 'What sort of services?' The idea sounded fantastic—a pipe dream surely?

'Do you know much about the internet and the worldwide web?'

'A bit. We set up a system at the library last year.'

'Then you'll know what a URL is.'

'An address on the internet.'

'The Busiatan king's eldest son has persuaded his father and the island's governing council that Busiata could provide a global internet hosting service, particularly for businesses. Anyone anywhere around the globe could have their own website based on Busiata where they can advertise to anyone with a computer connected to the internet and the worldwide web— the sites could even be designed there.'

'I know you can communicate with computers anywhere in the world, but why would people who don't live there choose to use an internet site on Busiata, of all places?'

'Commercial internet addresses usually end in 'co' or 'com' followed by the internet country code like u-k or n-z or a-u. Registered names can't be duplicated, so some firms are forced to use variations that their customers have problems remembering or finding. If they use a different country code from one that's already in use, they can register under their own name.'

'So?'

'The Busiatan suffix is b-u.'

'For Busiata—and for business?'

'That's it. And as electronic communications become more widespread there could be other services the Busiatans can provide via the internet. Part of my brief is to set up training and job opportunities for the locals.'

'That's…interesting,' Stefanie said dubiously.

'It's not as wacky as you might think. The island is already provided with satellite dishes and solar power, and the government hopes to attract back some of their nationals working overseas in communications. I've done a feasibility study and it looks promising.'

'Well, good luck. Busiata sounds idyllic.' Stefanie couldn't help a wistful note entering her voice. The thought of half a year on a tropical island far, far away from everything familiar had a definite attraction.

'Noelle didn't think so.' Quinn's expression turned grimly cynical.

'She didn't say anything about going overseas after…after you were married.'

'It was all confidential until the offer was firm. I asked her not to tell anyone. And she probably still hoped to talk me out of it. I admit I'd hoped to talk her *into* the idea. It's ironic, the way things have turned out…'

'What do you mean?'

Quinn's mouth twisted wryly. 'By leaving me she's very likely ditched my chance of getting the Busiatan assignment. In fact I half suspect that she might turn up again when she knows I've lost the contract, and expect me to take her back.'

Puzzled, Stefanie asked, 'Why would you lose it?'

'The king insists that the person who is given the tender has to be married. I told them I would be by the time I got to Busiata. The other candidate on the short list has a wife and three kids. This might just shift the balance. They've verbally offered me the contract, but nothing's been signed yet.'

'Surely they can't make conditions like that these days? It's archaic!'

'Busiata is a self-governing kingdom. They can make whatever conditions they like.'

'Why would you have to be married?'

'I imagine so that I'm unlikely to be tempted by the local maidens. Busiata is a very religious society. Way back in the nineteenth century, a missionary called Thomas Burford converted the present king's great-grandfather to Christianity, and of course the whole island followed. They frown on sex outside marriage. I gather they had a crop adviser from Australia there a few years back when they started a state-owned coffee plantation on the island, and the consul was a bit vague, but there was some sort of scandal involving the king's youngest sister.'

So they understandably didn't want a repeat. And one look at Quinn Branson would have rung alarm bells for the consul. Even when she'd been firmly committed to Bryan and he'd had eyes only for Noelle, it hadn't escaped Stefanie that he was the kind of man women instinctively recognised as an Alpha male, who would attract female attention without even trying. Heavens, she could feel a stirring of attraction herself, even now. Feminine instinct, she guessed—a natural reaction to obvious male virility, even though she was certainly not interested in finding a new man. Was Quinn still harbouring hopes of Noelle?

'Do you really think Noelle intends to come back?' she asked.

Quinn shrugged. 'Frankly, I don't care what her plans are. I'm not going to stick around to find out.'

'Even if you don't get the contract?'

His eyes briefly flashed before he bit into a sandwich. He swallowed a mouthful, then said, 'Especially if I don't get the contract. Damn her,' he added dispassionately.

'But if you love her…'

'You said you love Bryan. What would you do if he asked you to take him back?'

It was a fair question, she supposed, even if it did make her wince. 'I don't know. But if he's in love with Noelle…he won't ask, will he?'

He regarded her interestedly, almost speculatively. 'Am I opening wounds?'

'It's all right. We're both still raw, I guess.' She looked away from him again to hide the tears that threatened.

Unexpectedly, he reached across the narrow space between them and laid a hand over hers, his fingers strong and warm. 'We'll weather it. Give it time.'

'Yes.' She recalled saying something of the sort to him when he'd come to see her on what should have been her wedding eve. 'But it doesn't really help much now, does it?'

Quinn gave a tiny nod of acknowledgement and withdrew his hand. 'What are you doing tonight?'

'Tonight?' Stefanie blinked. 'Why?'

'Someone pressed a couple of free tickets on me for a symphony concert. I was intending to give them away—going to a concert alone seems hardly better than sitting in my hotel room with a glass of whisky and a book. Perhaps you and a friend could use them…'

'I'm avoiding my friends right now.'

'Well, if you don't have other plans, maybe you'd care to accompany me…or is the Symphonia not your kind of music?'

She too was facing another evening alone, in her room at her cheap hotel. 'I had planned to wash my hair,' she deadpanned, 'but I'd enjoy a good concert. If you're sure you want to take me.'

He was silent for a moment and she couldn't read his expression—it was almost as if he were thinking of something else. Or regretting the offer. Then he said, 'I want to. Can I pick you up? Tell me where to find you.'

Stefanie dressed for the concert with a mild sense of anticipation. It didn't remove the leaden weight that seemed to have taken up permanent residence in her chest, but it did lighten it. Maybe she should make the effort to go out more. Only she scarcely knew anyone in Wellington, which was precisely why she'd chosen to come here, and as Quinn had suggested, going alone to an occasion where most people were with someone would simply have increased her sense of isolation.

Filling in time, she applied makeup with more than usual care, and slipped on a pale apricot synthetic dress that looked like silk but didn't crush, and was the sort of garment that could go anywhere. She had actually washed her hair, and now, dried and brushed to a sheen, it hung to her shoulders, straight and fine and with the light waywardness of being newly washed.

She went down to the hotel foyer and found a chair in a corner by a polished table near the reception desk. Soon afterwards the door was pushed open and Quinn entered, dressed in a dark suit and white shirt. She stood up, catching his eye, and couldn't help noticing that a couple of other women were staring enviously as he came over to her swiftly, his stride long and easy.

For an instant she saw him through their eyes, a handsome, sexy stranger. The faint stirring of her blood reminded her that Bryan's wounding betrayal hadn't killed all her sexual feelings. She was still capable of an instinctive female response to a man like Quinn. Of course it didn't mean anything but it should give her some hope for a future without Bryan.

Quinn smiled as he reached her. 'Have you been waiting long?'

'No, you're dead on time,' she assured him as they walked to the door, his hand lightly touching her elbow. 'I came down early.'

Outside, he opened the door of a waiting taxi for her. After sliding in beside her and giving the driver directions, he turned and said, 'You look very nice.'

'You don't have to give me compliments, Quinn. We're just keeping each other company.'

'Does that preclude compliments? You do look nice and I thought you might like to be told so. And I'm very glad you decided to keep me company.'

Stefanie briefly caught her lower lip in her teeth. He was offering a boost to her inevitably wounded ego and she had rebuffed him. 'I didn't mean to be ungracious. It was kind of you to ask me out.'

'Not kind at all—it was purely selfish. Why don't

we try to forget about…what brought us together, and concentrate on enjoying ourselves?'

To her mild astonishment, Stefanie did enjoy herself. Sitting in the darkened concert hall, she allowed the music to wash over her, and for a short time actually was able to forget the constant ache of the loss of all she'd dreamed of for months, and push away the memory of humiliation and heartbreak. When the concert was over she was reluctant to leave her seat and return to the real world.

In the crush of the departing crowd Quinn's hand left her arm and rested on her waist while they made their way towards the door. It felt protective and rather pleasant. More than pleasant, she admitted to herself honestly. Pleasurable.

Outside the air was cool and fresh. Quinn dropped his hand from her and asked, 'Shall we get a coffee and something to eat before I take you back to your hotel?'

Not sure if he was just being polite, she turned to look at him, but could read nothing in his face. 'If you'd like it,' she said hesitantly. 'But I can get a taxi.'

'It's no bother. And I'd like a coffee at least. If that's okay?'

'That's fine. Thank you.'

They had coffee and desserts, and talked about the performance and their musical tastes. Hers were more eclectic than his rather selective preferences, but they found mutual ground on a number of composers of both popular and classical pieces.

When the bill came Stefanie offered to pay since he'd provided the concert tickets, but Quinn reminded her, 'The tickets were free. I appreciate the gesture but it would make me feel cheap.'

'Well, thank you,' she said. 'I've had a very pleasant evening.'

'So have I,' he told her. 'I guess the old cliché is true. Life goes on, doesn't it?'

She supposed it did, in some fashion. And one day she might feel normal, even happy. Again she felt a stirring of elusive, distant hope.

Despite her protest he accompanied her to her hotel, and there was an awkward little moment at the main door when she said goodnight, not knowing whether to offer him her hand because it seemed too formal, and yet anything else would be too intimate. Then he leaned over and pushed the big swinging door open for her. 'Good luck with the job hunting,' he said. 'See you.'

She walked past him and he gave her a tight smile, a nod, and let the door swing shut again.

So that was that, she told herself, ignoring the creaking old elevator and making her way up the wide, shabbily carpeted stairs to her room. She was glad she'd accepted the invitation. Only now she felt distinctly flat.

The next day when she came back at four from another fruitless day of interviews with bored personnel managers, the hotel receptionist told her, 'There were some calls for you, Miss Varney.'

Stefanie took the slips of paper, expecting to see messages from her family or, hopefully, from prospective employers. Instead both informed her that Mr Branson had telephoned, and one had a number for her to return the call.

In her room she eased off her shoes and dropped her shoulder bag on the bed, then placed the message slips by the bedside phone and sat down to massage her aching stockinged feet. Wellington pavements were hard. The city's notorious wind had played havoc with her hair too. She'd pulled the fine strands back in a smooth pleat this morning, but now several wisped about her face in tangled tendrils.

She recalled that on balmy days the city was beautiful in its way. Quaint old houses marched up its steep surrounding hills, and stood cheek by jowl alongside exciting new architectural forms around the gracefully curved shore of Oriental Bay, a snug haven of blue water. But the wind could be vicious, and battling it had made her tired and cranky. All she wanted was a warm shower and a light meal followed by an evening curled up with a good book.

She was stepping out of the shower when the telephone shrilled. Hastily she wrapped a towel about her body and hurried to the phone, leaving wet footprints on the carpet.

At her 'Hello?' a vibrant male voice said, 'Stefanie? Quinn. Did you get my messages?'

'Yes, I was going to call you back later.'

'Is this a bad time? I didn't want to miss you.'

'It's all right. But I've just had a shower and I'm dripping.'

'Sorry, I'll keep it short. Have you found a job?' he asked abruptly.

'No,' Stefanie answered, wondering why he sounded so urgent.

'Then can you meet me tonight? I have something to run by you, and I'd rather we talked face to face.'

'A job?' she asked.

For a moment she thought they'd been cut off. Then Quinn said slowly, 'Let's say...a possibility. Why don't we have dinner and I'll tell you about it?'

What did she have to lose, after all? 'All right,' she said, 'but this time I'll pay for myself.'

'We'll talk about that when you've heard my...proposition. Where would you like to go?'

'You choose. I'll meet you.'

A short pause. 'Would you mind coming to my hotel? They do a good meal, and I can get us a quiet table so we can talk.'

'All right. Where are you?'

It was a whole lot more upmarket than her own modest lodging, she thought, writing it down, along with the time he suggested. 'I'll be there,' she promised. 'Goodbye.'

She put on a cotton dress and jacket. After being on her feet all day she was glad to slip into a comfortable pair of low-heeled shoes, but almost regretted that choice when Quinn rose from the leather chair in the lobby of his hotel where he'd been reading a newspaper and came towards her. He seemed even taller, and the hard, enigmatic outlines of his face verged on intimidating.

Then he smiled at her and the stern planes of cheekbone and jaw relaxed. 'Thanks for coming,' he said. 'Would you like a drink in the bar first?'

They sat at a tiny table on deep chairs. After she'd answered his enquiry about the kind of day she'd had and a waitress had brought them drinks, Stefanie took a sip through the pink-striped straw of the cocktail she'd asked for and said, 'Why did you want to see me?'

'Later,' he said. 'I'm hoping to soften you up with good food and strong drink first.'

'That sounds sinister.' She echoed his light tone.

'It's not sinister, just...unusual.'

He wasn't going to satisfy her curiosity yet, she could see. 'Did you see your consul?' she asked him.

'Yes.' He picked up his beer and swallowed some.

'What did he say about your not getting married after all?'

'Nothing. We're still negotiating on a couple of points.'

'And that's one of them?'

'As a matter of fact,' Quinn said, 'I haven't told him yet.'

'Oh?' He didn't seem the sort of man to put things off. Or to deliberately deceive. 'Do you plan to tell them before or after you sign the contract? And if you don't say anything, won't that make it null and void or something?'

'I'm hoping I won't need to tell them.'

Stefanie wasn't sure what to say. She stirred her drink with the straw before taking another sip. 'Are you,' she said carefully, 'still hoping that Noelle might come back to you?'

She heard him take in his breath. Then he paused, as if changing his mind about what he was going to say. 'You're close friends, aren't you?' he asked. 'Or were.'

'We've known each other since kindergarten.'

'Do you think she'll come back?'

'I don't know.' Stefanie bent her head and finished her drink, then glanced at Quinn. 'She's always been rather...undecided about men.'

'Fickle, you mean.' He sounded cynical.

'I thought she just hadn't found the right one. She'd been pretty much spoiled for choice, you know.'

'I'll bet.' There was another pause before he said, 'Did you think I was the right man for her?'

Stefanie looked at him candidly. In hindsight it would be easy to say no. On first meeting him she had thought his protective and slightly possessive strength might be just what Noelle needed to make her feel secure—her father had left her mother when Noelle was five, and maybe she'd been looking for someone to take his place all her life. But Noelle wasn't a strong-willed person, and Quinn's decisive personality might have overwhelmed her.

Cautiously she answered, 'I didn't know you well enough to say. Noelle seemed happy, and I could see you were in love with her.'

He moved restlessly, as though the reminder embarrassed him. 'I told you I'm not waiting around for Noelle to change her mind,' he said shortly. 'That still holds. And you did say that you wouldn't want Bryan back, didn't you?'

'Not exactly.' She'd said she wouldn't want to marry someone who was in love with another woman, but she let his interpretation pass. 'I certainly wouldn't marry him now.'

Quinn put down his emptied glass with a muffled thud. 'Right,' he said. 'We could go to our table, unless you'd like another drink?'

Stefanie shook her head. 'I'm ready to eat.' She was quite hungry—all that walking about the city streets, she guessed. It was a while since she'd taken any real interest in food.

And the food they ate was superb. When they'd had their main course and she'd turned down a sweet in favour of sharing a cheeseboard with Quinn, she looked up with a smile as the waiter took the menus away. 'Well, if you wanted to soften me up, as you said, I must say you've made a great job of it. That was delicious. The wine is good too.'

She hadn't drunk a lot of the bottle he'd ordered, but it was enough to flush her cheeks and relax her quite nicely. She'd regaled Quinn with the story of her abortive interviews, and he'd laughed aloud at her slightly exaggerated, mournful account of failure, as she'd intended him to. Seeing him laugh properly had lit a tiny spark of warmth inside her.

Maybe they were good for each other. She half wished that someone from Ratanui might just happen by. They would see that she wasn't languishing in some dim corner with her broken heart, but enjoying dinner with a handsome man in a classy restaurant.

'What are you thinking?' Quinn asked her.

'That this is what I needed,' she said simply, slicing a piece of creamy Havarti and placing it on a cracker. 'But we haven't got down to business, have we? What did you want to talk to me about?'

Quinn helped himself to a wedge of Taranaki Blue Vein and put it on his plate. Then he looked up. 'I'm not sure how to put this. The thing is, Stefanie—I want to ask you to marry me.'

CHAPTER THREE

THE slice of cheese slid off the cracker Stefanie had halfway to her mouth. 'Pardon?' Her fingers shaking, she placed the cracker carefully back on the plate.

Quinn gave her a crooked grin. 'Maybe I should have led up to it.'

'Maybe you should,' she agreed faintly, staring at him. 'You're not serious!' But surely he wouldn't joke about it? Was he so distraught at Noelle's leaving him that he'd actually slipped a cog in his brain? He didn't *seem* distraught; in fact she'd thought he was extremely controlled and contained, but...

Warily she returned his scrutiny, trying to see behind the neutrally alert expression.

'I'm not crazy,' he assured her calmly. 'Only I told you about my problem with the Busiatan contract. And last night I got to thinking...about your difficulty finding work, and your understandable desire to escape your well-meaning friends and family. And the answer was right there. It's perfectly obvious.'

'It is?'

'Think about it. Of course it wouldn't be a real marriage in the accepted sense—'

'You mean you want me to *pretend* to be your wife?'

He hesitated. 'I can't deceive my employers to that extent, and they may ask for documentation. We'd have to have a marriage certificate. It only takes three days to get a licence and arrange the ceremony. Just enough time. I already have two plane tickets. Do you have a passport?'

'Yes.' She'd got one when she'd holidayed in Australia last year. 'But this is…we can't!'

'Why not?'

'For one thing, we hardly know each other!'

'I don't expect the usual marital privileges. It would be more like sharing a flat with someone. I can give you character references if you're worried I might take advantage of the situation.'

She didn't need that reassurance. Even if he hadn't still been in love with Noelle, from the little she knew of him that sort of danger seemed unlikely. But of course it was irrelevant, because there was no way this would work.

'Look on it as a job offer,' he urged. 'It's only for the duration of my contract with the Busiatan government—that's six months. We can draw up a pre-marital agreement, setting out the terms.'

'Terms?'

'I'll give you a small wage on the island and a lump sum—call it a severance payment—when we come back to New Zealand, and two years from then we can legally divorce. If you meet someone else that isn't so long to wait, is it?'

'You *are* serious!' He had thought it through. What was more, he was making it sound almost like a normal business arrangement.

Quinn leaned forward, his forearms on the table, his hands loosely linked. They were good hands, the fingers long but blunt-ended with short-cut nails—strong-looking although he wasn't a manual worker. She recalled how firm and warm his brief comforting clasp had been at lunch yesterday, and the light reassurance of his palm against her back as he ushered her from the theatre last night.

He said, 'I don't want to lose this assignment over a technicality that has nothing to do with my ability to carry out the job I'm being hired for.'

'You seem to be doing all right.' She looked about them at the luxurious trappings of the hotel.

'Window-dressing,' he said dismissively. 'Looking successful gives clients confidence.'

'Really?' She supposed it made sense.

'So far I'm working from my flat, with a part-time accountant to do the books. The money from the Busiatan contract will be enough to set me up in a proper office and employ a small staff. The salary is extremely good, and accommodation and travel are taken care of.'

'I suppose it's difficult to persuade computer consultants to live on a tiny Pacific island for months on end.'

'I rather thought you envied me yesterday.'

He was very astute. 'Yes, I did.'

'Then give some thought to this. Half a year at least on a beautiful tropical island, with no strings, and at the end of it enough to keep you for the next six months while you find yourself a real job.' His smile was persuasive, his eyes brilliant, and she wondered if he was deliberately pouring on the charm. If he'd smiled like that at Noelle, how had she even thought about another man? Right now Stefanie was finding it difficult to think sensibly about anything.

She said, 'It's such a wild idea, getting married for—well…under false pretences.'

'Marriages of convenience aren't so rare. People do it to avoid taxes, to gain residency, to hide their sexual orientation—for all kinds of reasons. As for false pretences, the stipulation is I must be legally married. What happens—or rather, doesn't happen—within the marriage needn't concern anyone but us.'

That was a point, but the stipulation had been made because a married man was presumed not to be a sexual adventurer. She didn't think hiding his sexual orientation had been behind Quinn's intention to marry Noelle. She made an effort to regard him coolly. 'And what about the local maidens I'm supposed to be protecting you from? Or is it the other way round? Will you be able to handle six months of celibacy?'

His eyebrows twitched very slightly, the only sign of surprise. 'Will you?'

'Yes!' She definitely wasn't ready to plunge into another relationship so soon after the disastrous end to her engagement. Her cheeks heating, she kept her eyes resolutely on his face.

With quiet confidence he said, 'I wouldn't mess up this project by giving in to the lusts of the flesh, whether I was married or not.'

She couldn't help a small laugh at the colourful language. 'Is that how they view sex there?'

'I'm sure that's how the good Reverend Burford put it.'

'Have you delved into the island's history?'

'I heard a few stories while I was there. I believe the palace holds a collection of historical documents but I've never seen them.'

'There must be fascinating stuff in there.'

His eyes gleamed. 'Maybe you could persuade them to let you have a look.'

He wasn't missing a thing in his effort to sway her.

'Do you really think it would work?' she asked. 'A fake marriage?'

'It's not a fake,' he argued. 'Just a bit unusual. I wouldn't have asked you if I didn't think we could make a go of this, Stefanie.'

She cast him a look of open scepticism. 'The thing is, you're desperate to take a wife along on this assignment and I happen to be handy, that's all! It's no use trying to dress it up.'

He spread his hands away from his plate. 'No, that's not all. I do know other women who might have been prepared to help me out if I'd asked them, but it never occurred to me to do that. There are several reasons why I thought of suggesting it to you.'

'What reasons?' she asked suspiciously.

'For one thing, I'm not just begging a favour—you need a breathing space and I'm offering you one. And from my point of view you'd be ideal. You're used to living in a small, narrow community, you're intelligent enough to enjoy the stimulation of an exotic environment, and not likely to throw tantrums if things don't go according to plan. We've already discovered we have tastes in common and don't grate on each other. At least, I hope that's true for you, and if not you hide it well.'

'You don't grate on me,' Stefanie murmured as he paused, presumably to give her a chance to comment.

'And also,' he continued, 'we're both in the same...emotional situation, so...'

'So?' Stefanie prompted as he looked vaguely uncomfortable.

'So,' he said slowly, 'there's no danger of your misunderstanding the terms of agreement, and possibly getting hurt.'

And ultimately accusing him of leading her up the garden path? Any other woman—one who hadn't been recently jilted—might begin taking the relationship too seriously. With her he knew he was safe. 'I see,' she said.

'And not least, you're...eminently presentable.' His eyes flickered over her, making her skin tingle.

'Presentable?'

'We'll be socialising with the royal family and local dignitaries. It comes with the job. I've noticed you have very good manners. The king and his family are fairly conscious of their dignity, and so are his people.'

'Would I have to curtsey or something?'

'Nothing like that, just show them normal respect, and make some effort to fit in with local custom. I don't think you'd be likely to do anything that would offend them. Any man would be proud to introduce you as his wife.'

'I haven't said I'm going to—'

'You don't need to give me an answer tonight,' he assured her. 'Think it over. I have a feeling you're not the type of person to leap into a situation without considering all the angles. But try a bit of lateral thinking. Maybe you'll come round to the idea.'

'You make me sound unadventurous and blinkered.'

'I didn't mean that. Caution is a commendable thing. But sometimes it can stop us from doing things we might enjoy—or at least find interesting.'

'And you think I'd find Busiata interesting.'

'I think you would.' As if it had just occurred to him, he added, 'You're not much like Noelle, are you? How did you two stay such close friends?'

'We've known each other for ever, and I suppose we're both...loyal.' Even though their interests had diverged as they grew older, they'd always kept in touch. After Noelle's family moved to Auckland when she was fifteen, she had often spent time in the school holidays with Stefanie's family, and Stefanie had stayed with Noelle when visiting the city.

Quinn's brows rose. 'Noelle—loyal?'

'I know she's let you down,' Stefanie acknowledged. 'Let down both of us, really. But that doesn't make her wicked or vindictive. She's never been a very strong-minded person.'

'That's remarkably tolerant of you.'

'I've been angry,' she admitted. 'With both of them. But what's the point? You know, it wasn't wrong of them not to go through with the weddings once they realised they were mistaken about...us. They could have chosen a better way to do it, but what difference would it have made in the end? We were still going to be hurt. I guess they just didn't want to be there to see it.'

'They just wanted to be together, according to my ex-beloved.'

She looked up at him and saw bitter anger in his eyes. 'Well, at least someone's happy. None of us would have been if they hadn't pulled the plug.'

'You're a very pragmatic soul, aren't you?' His gaze became speculative and his voice, she thought, slightly jeering.

'That seems to be what you want at the moment,' she reminded him rather crisply. 'Isn't pragmatism what your proposition is all about?'

'True.' He pushed away his plate. 'Do you want

anything more?'

Stefanie shook her head. 'I'm ready to go.'

She hardly slept, turning over Quinn's astonishing proposal in her mind all night, repeatedly telling herself she couldn't possibly agree.

In the morning she got up early as usual and quickly dressed, going downstairs to collect a morning paper and take it into breakfast with her.

But the columns of 'Situations Vacant' seemed to dance before her eyes. Outside it was raining, and she kept hearing the echo of Quinn's deep voice: *A beautiful tropical island…try a bit of lateral thinking…*

And despite his protest that he hadn't meant to, he'd implied she was overcautious, unlikely to do anything on impulse. 'Translation: dull and unexciting,' she murmured to herself.

She'd lived in one admittedly pleasant and quite lively place practically all her life, spending only a short period in Wellington getting her library qualification, and had planned to marry her hometown sweetheart. Bryan had taken his law degree in Auckland, but after the wedding he had expected to join his father's legal practice in Ratanui. He and Stefanie would have moved into a rented house in the town when they returned from their honeymoon, while they continued saving for their own home.

She'd envisaged eventually leaving her library job to have Bryan's children, and perhaps returning to work when they were old enough—a life not too different from her parents' happy marriage. All wholly predictable and ordinary.

None of it was going to happen, she reminded herself, brushing toast crumbs off the newsprint in front of her. At least, not with Bryan.

The most adventurous thing she'd ever done was

take a holiday in Australia, a short hop across the Tasman, with Noelle and another girlfriend.

She turned a page, refolded the paper, and picked up her ballpoint to ring a small ad for 'Personable young people for market research'. Then crossed it out when she saw the last sentence. 'Must have own car and phone.'

A picture of a palm tree caught her eye, boxed inside a travel advertisement in a corner of the page. A man and a woman, wearing minimal clothing, stood hand in hand under the palm, gazing at a quiet lagoon. 'Bargain Tropical Holidays,' the caption read. 'Seven Days in Vanuatu.'

One week. Quinn had offered her six months in a similar idyllic setting. She could be crazy not to snatch at the chance.

Dragging her attention from the picture, she ran her gaze down the adjacent columns. Shop assistant... Tea-maker... Undertaker's assistant. She shuddered. Washing machine repairer, experienced... Waiter... Well-driller... Window-cleaner... Young women, attractive, for massage parlour...

Stefanie grimaced, finished her coffee, and took the paper up to her room.

The phone was ringing when she opened the door. She rushed to pick up the receiver, and her mother's voice said, 'Stef? Are you all right? I phoned last night and you weren't in.'

'I went out to dinner,' Stefanie explained.

'Oh, really?' Patti's anxiety changed to pleased surprise. 'With a man?'

Anticipating all kinds of questions if she gave the details, Stefanie tried to seem nonchalant and dismissive. 'Yes, but it wasn't a date. It was about a job, actually.'

'A job? And he took you out to dinner? That sounds just a teeny bit suspicious to me.'

'It's all right, I'm not stupid, Mum.'

'Of course not, darling. Only you're in a vulnerable state right now—you will be careful, won't you?'

'I'm always careful,' Stefanie assured her. And what had that got her? asked a jeering inner voice. Certainly not the happy, conventional life she'd planned.

'I wish you'd come home,' Patti fretted. 'Don't you think you'd feel better among people who care about you?'

'No,' Stefanie said under her breath, mentally recoiling.

'What, dear?'

'I don't want to be an object of pity.'

'Oh, I wouldn't call it pity. Everyone's concerned about you, asking after you. There's not much sympathy for Bryan and Noelle. Um…they're back, you know, living together right here in Ratanui!' Her voice rose indignantly. 'I must say I'm surprised. I heard Noelle's actually going to work in Bryan's family's firm. The receptionist left to have a baby, and Noelle's taking her place!'

Stefanie felt her hand go damp and slippery on the receiver. 'That will be nice for them.'

Patti gave a delicate little snort. 'I don't know how they dared show their faces here! Everyone's on your side, of course.'

'I know I should be grateful, but I wish they'd all forget about it.'

'Oh, I'm sure they will soon. What sort of job was this man offering you? Are you going to take it?'

'I haven't decided. It's on Busiata. A...a government job.'

'On what?'

'Busiata—you know, in the Pacific.'

'The *island*? But it's *miles* from anywhere!'

'That's the attraction,' Stefanie said patiently. Why was she telling her mother this? She hadn't agreed to Quinn's preposterous proposal and she had no intention of actually going to Busiata...did she? 'As I said, I haven't decided.'

'How long would you be there? Would you have to get there by trading boat or something?'

'I think they have an air service. The job's only for six months.'

With a small shock she realised that somehow talking to her mother had made the whole thing seem more real, more possible, although she was keeping back the most vital, salient element.

'I don't think I like the sound of it,' Patti said firmly. 'Is it some kind of office job? You'd be bored, wouldn't you?'

Curiously, Stefanie felt perversely driven to defend the idea. 'I don't think so. Pacific islands are very beautiful. And Busiata's quite safe—the people are strictly religious. Besides, I gather I'd be sort of under the patronage of the Busiatan royal family.'

'Oh. Well, I don't know...'

'I'm not ready to come home yet.' She'd half hoped Bryan would remain in Auckland after all— the small-town gossip would be tough on him and Noelle—but she supposed his father was relying on his promise to join the family firm. And Bryan wouldn't have lined up any other job.

And now more than ever she didn't want to go back there.

After she'd hung up she sat staring at the paper in her hand, studying the ads she'd circled. None of them really appealed.

Rain hurled itself against the window panes and ran down the glass in crooked little rivulets, blurring the grey buildings across the road. In a narrow gap between two of the buildings, a tree top lashed about in the wind.

If she phoned any of these numbers she'd have to go out into that weather.

Again the picture of the couple on the tropical island caught her eye. Palm trees, blue seas. Warmth. And no pressure, no need to hide. The only person who would know what had happened to her was the one person in the world who shared her own bewilderment and anger and heartache, who fully understood.

Where had she put the slip of paper with Quinn's number on it?

She found it under the telephone book and dialled swiftly, before she had time to think of all the reasons she shouldn't do this. For once in her life she was going to do something rash and unpredictable.

When he answered on the third ring she took a deep breath. 'It's Stefanie,' she said. 'About that proposition…'

CHAPTER FOUR

EVERYTHING moved so fast after that, Stefanie scarcely had time to think. Quinn applied for a marriage licence and made an appointment at the registry office. He measured Stefanie's finger with a piece of string, so that he could buy a ring. She was relieved that he was taking care of that, because choosing one together—it would have been such a farce.

They spent hours together in cafés, walking about the hilly streets or sitting on a park seat at Oriental Bay, exchanging information on their families, their education, jobs—things that a newly wed couple would presumably know about each other.

Leaning on a railing overlooking the harbour, Stefanie asked him, 'Do you have brothers or sisters?' He'd mentioned none, only telling her that his parents had farmed in the Wairarapa for many years and now ran a small mail-order seed business.

When he didn't answer immediately she turned her head to look at his strong profile, only slightly mellowed by the way the wind blew his hair over his forehead as he watched a ferry come into the harbour. His eyes fixed on the distant craft, he said, 'I had a younger sister but she died.' He showed no sign of emotion, his voice cool and expressionless.

'I'm so sorry! That's very sad,' she said.

'It was a long time ago,' he said dismissively. 'I was just a kid.'

Stefanie tried to imagine how she would feel if she

lost one of her beloved sisters, the very thought chilling her, sending a rising tide of fear through her entire body, making her feel she wanted to contact them right now, assure herself they were both all right. She knew if anything happened to Gwenda or Tracey, she'd be devastated. No way would she be able to speak of them in the cool, dispassionate way that Quinn had so casually mentioned his dead sister.

But he'd said it was a long time ago. Probably he'd been too young to clearly remember much about his only sibling. 'Was it a cot death?'

'No,' Quinn said. 'But she had something wrong with her from birth.'

She'd died as a baby, Stefanie guessed. He had never really known his sister, then. 'It must have been hard for your parents,' she said.

'Yes. It still is.' He straightened, and took her hand in his. 'I could do with a coffee. There's a café just down the road there—look all right to you?'

On the night before their appointment at the registry office they dined in a cosy Wellington restaurant. Stefanie was distracted, hardly caring what she ate, trying to concentrate on the snippets of information Quinn was giving her, background that would be useful to her when they got to Busiata.

Instead she found herself studying Quinn. She watched the movement of his throat when he drank the ruby-red wine he'd ordered, and the way he curled his entire hand about his coffee cup instead of threading one long, blunt finger through the handle. Every detail seemed to etch itself on her mind, from the shadowy patch at the corner of his chin that he'd missed when shaving to the way his hair escaped from its combed-back style as he bent over his meal, sending strands flopping across his forehead until he flicked them impatiently back with his fingers. He turned his head to summon a waiter, and she was struck by the length of his dark lashes, and when he caught her looking at him and lifted a questioning eyebrow, she responded to the amused glint in his eye with a strange lift of her heart, and felt herself flush.

Each time they met she was more vividly aware that he was a very attractive male. But it had been at first an objective judgement, not an emotional reaction. Subtly, something had changed. Perhaps because in the last few days they'd been spending so much time together.

In the taxi on the way back to her hotel, although he sat a good foot from her, she could faintly smell Quinn's male scent—soap or aftershave, clean shirting and something uniquely his—and when they passed under a streetlamp her heart gave a lurch of something like trepidation as she saw his profile momentarily etched in stark relief, the harsh outlines of brow and nose, mouth and chin as if carved from granite. What did she really know of him?

She had agreed to live in a situation of artificial intimacy with this near-stranger, and maybe that was what was making her super-aware of him. Tonight was her last chance to back out of this bizarre bargain.

A momentary panic threatened to take hold of her, the jumping pulse at the base of her throat a sign of nervous tension.

At the end of the journey he told the driver to wait, and escorted her to the hotel door, a hand firmly circling her arm. For a fanciful second or two it seemed as if she were his prisoner.

When they reached the top of the steps she turned to him, almost ready to blurt out that she'd changed her mind, that she wasn't prepared, after all, to travel thousands of miles to live side by side with a man she barely knew.

Then he said, 'You're scared, aren't you? Just remember, it's only a job. And if you find you can't take it on Busiata I suppose I could always send you home.'

'Wouldn't they terminate your contract?'

'It does state my wife must be living with me for the duration—but once I've started on the job I doubt they'd hold us to that.'

They might. And it was too late for him to find someone to replace her. If she let him down now he'd have no one left to turn to.

As she hesitated he took her other arm, drawing her a little closer so that he could see her face. 'I won't keep you against your will, Stefanie. But I hope you're going to like the island. It's the nearest thing to Paradise I've ever seen.'

He'd shown her pictures of tall coconut palms, white beaches and blue seas, smiling brown-skinned people. Most women would think her mad to think of turning down the chance to spend time there while her heart healed. In fact most women might have leapt at it when Quinn first broached the subject.

His thumbs moved absently on her arms. 'Okay?' he murmured, his eyes finding hers in the light spilling from the hotel foyer.

Stefanie swallowed. 'Okay,' she agreed. If she chickened out now she'd despise herself for ever as a coward who had let a once-in-a-lifetime opportunity slip from her fingers.

'Terrific.' Unexpectedly he bent and brushed a kiss against her forehead before releasing her. 'I'll pick you up tomorrow.'

She dithered over what to wear, wishing she'd bought something new, and yet conscious that this was no ordinary wedding. She still hadn't told her family about that part of the deal, knowing her mother would be dismayed and anxious, and probably insist on flying to Wellington to dissuade her. And she felt guilty about the deception, but reminded herself it wasn't a real wedding, just a legal form that had to be gone through so that she and Quinn could go to Busiata, much like getting a passport and visa.

In the end she put on her synthetic silk-look apricot dress and slid her feet into high-heeled cream shoes. She pinned up her hair, and then changed her mind, letting it fall loose. Should she have a hat?

It would only blow away. The rain had stopped, but gusty winds still attacked the tops of the trees, and when she looked down into the street she saw people leaning forward as they walked, clutching their coats and jackets around them.

She pulled a lined cream linen jacket from the wardrobe and put it on. The clock told her it was time to leave. She wanted to lick her lips, but remembered her carefully applied lipstick, and refrained.

Quinn was entering the main door when she reached the ground floor. He smiled at her and came swiftly to her side. 'Ready?'

'As ready as I'll ever be,' she said, trying to smile back.

'Your eyes look enormous,' he told her, and took her hand in a firm grip to lead her to the door. 'Don't worry. It'll soon be over.'

Too soon, she thought, grateful for the warmth and strength of his fingers as they gently squeezed hers.

Registry staff were their only witnesses, and the ceremony was basic, simple and quickly over. Still, she felt hypocritical. When it was Quinn's turn to speak his voice was low and harsh—and he didn't look at her, but down at their joined hands. Then he slid a narrow gold band onto her finger and she felt a small, cold shock. The action seemed irrevocable somehow, though she knew the ring was a lie, that this whole thing was false. Her fingers trembled, and Quinn closed his hand about hers again.

His eyes lifted, met hers, and for a moment time seemed to stop. His face was grave, his gaze steady and dark. Compelling, as if he was afraid she wanted to run away, and was trying to keep her there by the sheer force of his will.

The registrar beamed at them, pronouncing them husband and wife, and Quinn hesitated, then he cupped her chin in his free hand, bent and kissed her.

Expecting a mere brushing of lips, she was surprised that his mouth lingered for seconds, firm and warm on hers, while he held her.

Taken unawares, she found a disturbing tide of heat racing through her body before Quinn drew back and smiled down at her, his eyebrows quirking slightly upward when he met her widened eyes.

The registrar closed the book, the witnesses congratulated them and shook Quinn's hand, and they were ushered out.

On the street, Quinn said, 'The worst part's over.

You look as though you could do with a drink, Mrs Branson. Did you have breakfast?'

Stefanie shook her head, hiding an odd sensation in her midriff at his use of the title. 'I didn't even think about food this morning.' She'd been too strung up.

Quinn found a café and got sandwiches and muffins with coffee, urging her to eat.

Stefanie had a sandwich, and it awakened her appetite.

'Not much of a wedding breakfast, I'm afraid,' Quinn apologised. 'Maybe I should have found somewhere more fancy.'

'It wasn't a real wedding,' she objected. 'This is fine.' To prove it, she took a muffin and split it.

'I'm sorry to have put you through that.' Quinn's eyes searched hers. His voice low, he asked, 'Was it very hard for you?'

Certainly it hadn't been the wedding she'd planned only weeks ago. And he obviously realised she couldn't help comparing this morning's stark legal ritual with the lifelong vows she would have exchanged with Bryan in a flower-filled church, with her father to escort her down the aisle, her bridesmaids attending her, her mother and friends looking on. 'It's all right,' she said. 'It wasn't so bad.' It couldn't have been easy for him, either. Had he been thinking of Noelle when he slid his ring onto *her* finger?

At that, a peculiar hollowness seemed to settle in her chest. Maybe he'd been thinking of Noelle when he kissed her after the ceremony—closing his eyes and imagining Noelle had just vowed her love and life to him.

Noelle would have kissed him back instead of being stricken motionless with surprise.

Quinn glanced at his watch. They were flying out later that day. 'We'll pick up your things and then mine,' he said. 'If you have any last-minute shopping to do we could spare an hour or so.'

'I don't think I need anything more.' She'd done a bit of extra shopping, but had tried to keep her luggage minimal. 'I'd like to phone home before we take off.'

'Have you told them about this?'

'I said I had a job on Busiata, and got them to send some clothes and stuff down here for me. But they'll want to write to me, so...I guess I'll have to tell them if I'm going to be known as Mrs Branson.'

Quinn frowned thoughtfully. 'Busiata is a very conservative society, and they'd certainly wonder about a married woman keeping her own name. But...I have the impression your mother and your younger sister, anyway, may not be souls of discretion.'

It was true but, 'How do you know?'

'You've talked about them. You were the responsible older sister who looked after the younger ones, lent them a sympathetic ear and got them out of trouble. Gwenda's the practical, take-charge one who gets things done, and Tracey's at the emotional teenage stage. She's more like your mother, and I gather you and Gwenda take after your father.'

Stefanie hadn't realised she'd told him so much, or that he'd listened so carefully. She had never described her family in those words, but his assessment was basically correct. Tracey or her mother was likely to tell one other person in the greatest of confidence, and then be astonished and disbelieving that the secret had got out. 'I don't know what we can tell them,' she said, 'if I have to use your name.'

He glanced around as if looking for inspiration. 'Would your family accept that you married me on the rebound?'

'They'd certainly be surprised.' She'd never been the impulsive sort. 'And hurt that I hadn't invited them to the wedding. I'll have to let them know it's only a…a makeshift marriage.'

He frowned. 'I know the chances seem remote, but the more people who know the real story, the more likely that someone on Busiata will hear of it. Besides, I don't think you want it spread about Ratanui.'

The news would fuel gossip anyway, but she'd prefer people didn't know it was a purely practical pretend marriage. Still… 'Who's going to believe it's the real thing? Barely three weeks after…'

'It won't be the first time people have married within weeks of meeting. Come to think of it, we met months ago, and you've been in Wellington for a while. No one will know we haven't been seeing each other all that time. It's not impossible that we found mutual comfort in our sorrow and decided to marry. Or even that we were attracted to each other before, and relieved to be free to follow our mutual desire.'

'I guess not,' Stefanie agreed doubtfully. He had an amazing talent for making the outrageously unlikely seem perfectly normal and logical. 'But how do I explain not telling my family I was getting married?'

'It was a whirlwind courtship and a sudden decision,' he suggested. 'There was no time.'

'It took three days to get the licence,' Stefanie objected. 'They could easily have come down in that time.'

'Okay...' He thought for a minute, then snapped his fingers. 'You had a superstitious dread of being left in the lurch again so soon after your previous experience. They'd forgive you for that, wouldn't they?'

'I suppose it might work.' Certainly they would understand she didn't want to go through another trauma like that. 'Maybe they'd believe it.'

'Well,' he said, as if it were all settled, 'we'd better get moving. Do you want to make your phone calls from your hotel? Then I'll take care of the bill.'

'It's my bill. I pay my own way.'

'You're my wife now.'

'If I'm your wife, it's hardly appropriate for you to be paying me wages, then, except maybe a bit of housekeeping money.'

Slightly impatient, he said, 'Of course I'll pay—'

'Actually, Quinn, I really don't want to be paid for enjoying a tropical holiday.'

'It's part of the deal, Stefanie,' he said curtly.

'*I* never said so.' She'd turned down his offer of a prenuptial agreement, finding something tacky in formalising their strange bargain.

'I took it for granted—'

'Yes, it's a habit of yours.'

He looked angry and astonished at that, and she bit her lip, realising it hadn't been very tactful. But she refused to back down, meeting his gaze without flinching. 'I won't accept wages.'

Quinn took a deep breath and looked at her hard. 'All right,' he agreed reluctantly, 'but if you need money at any time while we're on Busiata, don't hesitate to ask.'

'I have some money,' she said, 'if I want to buy clothes or souvenirs.' It was to have gone towards her home, hers and Bryan's. What else would she spend it on, now?

'But you still get paid at the end—otherwise the deal's off.'

He looked as though he meant that. And if he was willing to compromise so should she be. Besides, she'd be coming back not having earned for six months unless she could find some sort of work on Busiata. She might need something to tide her over.

'Okay,' she said.

'You have a stubborn streak.' He sounded as if he'd just discovered something that didn't exactly please him.

'So do you,' she retorted. 'So don't throw stones.'

Only hours later they were on their way to Fiji, and then Busiata.

It wasn't necessary to make any part of the journey by cargo boat. After some time spent waiting in the transit lounge at Nandi, they boarded a much smaller plane with three other people and were flown across another vast expanse of blue ocean until a ring of turquoise surrounding a smudge of green became visible on the horizon, and soon they were circling the island, then coming in to land on a grassy airstrip.

The pilot let some steps down from the plane and helped Stefanie to the ground. The light was dazzling and the air humid and warm, laden with a faint scent of flowers.

Quinn came down the steps behind her and led her

to two long low buildings spanned by a single palm-thatched roof shading an intervening space where wooden benches provided cool seating.

A tall, wide-shouldered islander rose from one of the benches. He was dressed in a short-sleeved white shirt with epaulettes on the shoulders, khaki shorts and a peaked cap. Striding forward, he held out his hand to Quinn. '*Sambuda*, Mr Branson.'

'*Sambuda.*' Quinn returned the greeting and shook the large hand extended to him. 'Nice to see you again, Tipa. Stefanie, this is Tipa Bori, Prince Tuisani's driver. It's very kind of the prince to send you,' he added to the man.

Stefanie held out her hand, and had it engulfed in a large brown one. 'Hello, Mr Bori.'

He grinned at her. 'Everyone calls me Tipa, Mrs Branson. We'll wait for your luggage, and then we'll be on our way.'

The luggage was trundled over on a large cart, and Quinn and Tipa took the cases from it. Following them round the other side of the building, Stefanie blinked at the huge white limousine that stood there, polished and gleaming in the tropical sunlight. Nearby, other disembarked plane passengers were climbing into a battered minibus.

After the bags were stowed by the driver, she slid onto a long leather seat with Quinn beside her, and Tipa drove smoothly away from the airport.

Quinn looked down at her bemused expression and grinned. 'The royal family travels in style,' he murmured. 'But there's nowhere much to go on the island. I think this chariot spends most of its time sitting in the prince's garage.'

The narrow white road was bordered by dark green,

bushy plants and tall ferns. Two barefoot children on a horse urged their bony mount to the side as the car slowed to pass them. They waved and shouted the same greeting that Tipa had used at the airport. Stefanie waved back.

They came to a town where the road was wider and tarsealed, and Stefanie glimpsed shops and other buildings, some modest or even shabby, others double-storied and colonnaded. The main forms of transport seemed to be motor scooters and bicycles. The older women were uniformly encased in loose, long-sleeved printed floral dresses with skirts to their ankles, but some younger ones wore knee-length sarongs tucked about their breasts, and quite a number sported sleeveless tops with shorts or miniskirts. And both men and women had wreathed their glossy black hair with flowers.

'This is Iriata?' she asked Quinn.

'The capital, yes. That big building over there with the dome-shaped roof is Parliament House. Behind it and up the hill there you can just see part of the king's palace.' He leaned over to point it out to her, his arm momentarily resting on her shoulder, his cheek almost brushing hers.

Distracted by the faint masculine scent of his skin and the warm weight of his arm, she hardly saw the white building he indicated, partially obscured by tall palms.

Then they were winding uphill, past rows of houses, and through more trees brushing the roof of the limousine, finally going through a concrete-pillared gateway with no actual gate, and up a short drive between flowering shrubs before coming to a stop outside a white-painted stucco house with a terracotta-tiled roof.

The door opened as Quinn helped Stefanie from the car, and a middle-aged island couple came down the two broad steps.

The man, thin and wiry, was dressed similarly to Tipa but without the epaulettes and peaked cap, and the woman wore a colourful dress with a white apron tied about her substantial waist.

'I'm your housekeeper, Mrs Branson,' the woman explained. 'My name is Winnie. And this is Roari, my husband. He helps around the house and the garden.'

Stefanie threw a surprised, questioning glance at Quinn, but he just gave a tiny shrug before holding out his hand to Roari and then to the housekeeper. Hastily Stefanie followed suit, carefully pronouncing the local greeting as she smiled at the pair.

While Roari collected the heavy luggage, Winnie took Stefanie and Quinn along a cool passageway and threw open the door of a large, high-ceilinged room.

An enormous bed with polished brass ends dominated one wall, its pristine white cover heavily appliquéd with pastel-coloured flowers. There were two massive carved wardrobes and a matching dressing table, all in solid dark wood, and the polished board floor was softened by patterned mats.

'Your bedroom,' Winnie said. She crossed the room to another door between the two wardrobes and opened that onto a glimpse of shiny white tiles and a large porcelain basin with brass taps. 'Your bathroom.'

Quinn lowered the flight bags and computer case

he had carried, setting them down on the floor. Roari appeared in the doorway, laden with more luggage.

'Thanks,' Quinn said. 'Just put them down there.'

On her way to the door, Winnie said, 'Anything you want, let us know. The telephone is near the bed, there. Dial 9 for the kitchen, or 1 for an outside line. I'll make you some tea or cool drinks. Would you like them outside on the terrace or here? Fifteen minutes, all right?'

'That sounds good. The terrace,' Quinn suggested, glancing at Stefanie for confirmation. 'Cold drinks?'

She nodded, then waited until the couple had closed the door behind them before she blurted out, 'They expect us to sleep together!'

'Married couples usually do. Though in that bed we'd almost have to communicate by smoke signal.'

Stefanie refused to laugh. 'I am not sharing a bed with you!'

'All right,' he said easily. 'Only I don't want to make a big deal out of it to the housekeeper.'

'So what are we going to do?'

'Don't worry, we'll think of something.' He looked around, then strolled to the bathroom. She heard another door open and went to look.

The washbasin was almost big enough to bathe in, and featured enormous brass taps. An enormous old-fashioned bath sat on a dais at one side of the big bathroom, with a brass shower fitting over it.

'Looks like we have a solution,' Quinn said. 'Come and have a look.'

The door Quinn had opened on the other side of the bathroom led to another bedroom, and as he motioned her through she saw it was less opulent, with only one wardrobe and a smaller dressing table. The bed here was also a double, though not as generously proportioned, its headboard carved wood, and the cover similar to the one in the other room, with a different pattern of flowers.

'Which room do you want?' he asked her.

'This one's fine,' she said. 'Are you sure it's not in use? Winnie and Roari—'

'Winnie didn't say anything about us sharing the bathroom with anyone else. I'm sure this is a spare room.'

'When you told me the government was providing a house I didn't expect staff to come with it.'

'I thought I'd mentioned it.'

Could she have forgotten? She'd certainly been paying less than full attention the night before their wedding ceremony. Maybe she'd missed that bit. 'Do we need a housekeeper? With only the two of us I'm sure we can manage.'

'The house staff comes along with free rent. Jobs are scarce here, and the government creates employment wherever it can. We don't want to do anyone out of a livelihood.' Quinn strolled to the wardrobe and pulled open the door, revealing dark emptiness and a row of wire hangers. 'Are you sure you wouldn't prefer the bigger room?'

'No, thanks.' She hesitated. 'I suppose we'll have to think up some excuse to be using different rooms.' Not much use hoping they could keep their sleeping arrangements a secret from the housekeeper.

He turned and looked at her. 'I'll tell them I snore. And that my new bride is a light sleeper.'

'Do you?'

'Not to my knowledge—no one's ever complained.

But as an explanation it'll have to do. Unless you can think of something better.'

Stefanie shook her head. 'Thank you, Quinn.'

He gave her a narrow smile and came over to her, briefly lifting a hand to touch her cheek. 'I want you to be comfortable, Stefanie.' His eyes darkened. 'I know I stressed the advantages to you of this... situation, but you've helped me out and I'm grateful. I'll try to make things easy for you.'

He put his hand in his pocket and stepped back. 'I'll bring your bags through. Is that bed made up? We may have to ask Winnie to bring some sheets for you.'

She checked the bed while he was gone, and found obviously fresh sheets on it. After he brought her bags she said, 'I'd like a quick shower.' It had been a long trip and she felt stale and woolly-headed.

'Okay,' he said. 'Let me know when you've finished in the bathroom.'

It was just over five minutes before she knocked on the communicating door and called, 'It's all yours.'

As she changed into a cool, sleeveless yellow dress pulled from her suitcase, she heard the shower running again. Shortly after it had stopped Quinn knocked on her door. 'Stefanie? Are you ready?'

'Come in,' she invited him.

His hair was still damp, combed back. He'd shaved, and put on a slightly creased white cotton shirt, with easy-fitting light grey trousers. 'You look very fresh and sweet,' he told her approvingly. 'Like a daisy.'

If she were a daisy, Noelle would have been a lush pink rose. Stefanie pushed away the thought. She wasn't comparing him with Bryan, was she? Why should he compare her with his ex-fiancée?

They found Roari waiting at the end of the passageway. He escorted them to the rear of the house, where a wide terrace was shaded by a pergola threaded with leafy vines bearing vivid orange trumpets. On a wrought-iron table two tall glasses stood alongside a jug of pale golden liquid with ice cubes and lemon slices floating on top. As Stefanie and Quinn sat down Winnie appeared with a basket of still-warm cupcakes.

A palette-shaped swimming pool with clear, gleaming water lay invitingly only yards away, and leafy shrubs bordered the area, some of them bearing dazzling, brightly coloured flowers. The delicate, waxy blooms of a pink frangipani tree in one corner provided a sweet perfume that lingered in the warm, heavy air. After enquiring if there was anything else they would like, Winnie and Roari left them.

Stefanie gazed at the lush, unfamiliar surroundings and said, 'I feel as if I've strayed onto a movie set.'

Quinn laughed. 'I told you, Busiata is the nearest thing to Paradise.' He pushed the basket of cakes toward her. 'Try one of these. They're a local specialty.'

She took one and bit through the pale golden crust, finding the inside light and moist and coconut-flavoured. 'Delicious,' she said after swallowing the first mouthful. She picked up the glass that Winnie had filled before she left, and sipped at the chilled liquid. 'So is the juice.'

'Mango and lime, freshly made.'

'I think I could get used to this,' Stefanie admitted, savouring the sweet yet tart flavour.

'I hope so.' Quinn sat back in his chair, surveying her. His gaze slipped from her face, lingering with lazy appreciation on her bare arms, the scooped neckline of her dress. Then his eyelids drooped and he turned away, leaving her strangely disturbed.

He'd only recently lost his fiancée—a woman with far more obvious attractions than hers. A woman he'd been in love with. And Stefanie was still mourning her own lost love. So that couldn't have been desire she'd seen in his eyes, and of course it wasn't an answering sexual stirring that was making her heart thump and the blood run faster in her veins.

No, it was just...the unnatural situation, and her imagination working overtime.

But when Quinn lifted his glass and took a long draught she had to drag away her gaze from the firm curve of his throat rising from the open collar of his shirt, showing a vee of hard male chest.

He put down his glass. 'I have to see the Crown Prince tomorrow and bring him up to speed on my plans. Do you think you can amuse yourself for a few hours?'

'Don't worry about me. I have to write a letter to my family, and I'm sure I'll find plenty to do.' She had briefly broken the news before leaving Wellington that she and Quinn were married, assured them she was fine, and said she and her new husband had to catch a plane and she'd tell them all about the whirlwind decision later. It wasn't going to be an easy letter to write...

'I can see you're going to be very easy to live with.'

'You hardly know me yet.'

He smiled. 'I think I'm going to enjoy getting to

know you, Stefanie.' As Winnie appeared from the house and glided silently towards them, he added under his breath, his eyes holding a warning, 'And we'd better be careful what we say. You never know who might be around to hear it.'

CHAPTER FIVE

STEFANIE spent some time unpacking her things, and supposed that Quinn was doing the same. Then dusk fell with a suddenness that took her by surprise, and through the trees outside she could see lights pricking the darkness—a cluster that must have been the township, and other single lights or a few together scattered here and there among the thick trees.

'We must be quite high up,' she said to Quinn as they dined in a room that seemed too big for the two of them. Winnie had served them with a rice and fish combination accompanied by fresh cooked taro leaves.

The table was a long oval, but Winnie had set places on opposite sides of it.

'We're on the coolest part of the island. A lot of the government ministers have houses in the area. I believe this place belongs to a minor member of the extended royal family who spends most of his time in the States.'

Overhead a fan whirred faintly, creating a welcome waft of air. Stefanie was suddenly aware of how far from home she was, cocooned with a stranger who was her husband.

We're just living here together—like flatmates, she reminded herself—that was what Quinn had said. But somehow the false intimacy of sharing a meal seemed accentuated by the size of the room. Her nerve-ends quivered when Quinn reached across the table towards her, and then his fingers closed about the salt shaker and she mentally kicked herself for being stupid. He'd hardly looked at her since she entered the room. Obviously he wasn't as acutely aware of her as she was of him.

Stefanie swallowed a mouthful of subtly flavoured rice. When she spoke her voice was husky. 'It's a beautiful house.'

'I'm glad you like it.' The reflected lights glimmered in his eyes as he glanced up at her. 'That's a good start.'

'How do we get about the island?'

'A car will collect me each day, but motor vehicles on the island are strictly limited, except two-wheelers. Have you ever ridden a scooter?'

'I suppose I could learn,' she said dubiously.

'It's not hard. There are probably a couple in the garage, but wait until I can give you some lessons before you try them.'

'Do I need a driving licence?'

'Yes, but the test is easy. I'll organise it when I'm sure you won't kill yourself or anyone else.'

Which he would be the judge of, Stefanie supposed with a hint of resentment. 'I wouldn't even try if I thought I'd kill anyone,' she said.

There was laughter in his eyes as he leaned back a little in his chair, regarding her. 'Figure of speech,' he said soothingly. 'I suppose it's understandable if you're oversensitive at the moment.'

'I'm not oversensitive!'

He looked thoughtful. 'Then I'm sorry. I don't mean to rub you up the wrong way, Stefanie. We have to get along in this…situation.'

'I know. Maybe I am a bit…touchy right now,' she

allowed, more than willing to meet him halfway. 'And maybe you're trying to assert control over your life,' she guessed shrewdly. Noelle had upset his plans, thrown a spanner in the works, and he certainly hadn't liked it. 'I can understand that.'

Quinn seemed faintly startled, then his eyes narrowed. 'Can you, now?' he murmured. 'But you don't want me controlling yours, is that it?'

'In a nutshell.'

She smiled at him limpidly, and was rather relieved when he gave a short laugh. 'I can see I'd have my hands full if I tried,' he said.

After the first course Winnie brought in bowls of fruit salad and whipped cream, and Stefanie looked up to thank her. 'And the rice and fish was delicious,' she told the woman.

Winnie smiled and carried the used plates away.

When they'd finished Stefanie offered to help wash up, but the housekeeper looked quite shocked, vehemently declining before bustling away to the kitchen with a tray full of clattering crockery.

Quinn said, 'You did say you could get used to being waited on.'

'Well, it's not that easy. I'm beginning to feel lazy and pampered already.'

'Somehow I don't think you're lazy. You've every right to feel tired tonight, though. Don't let me keep you if you want to go up to bed.'

They had eaten later than she was accustomed to, although the time difference meant that she no longer had any idea what the hour would have been back home. It did seem to have been a long, eventful day, and her head felt a bit floaty. Just the mention of tiredness made her yawn. She lifted her hand to cover it. 'I think I will,' she said gratefully.

She read for a while after getting into bed, until the print began to dance before her eyes, and she put down the book and turned off the lamp that stood on a polished wooden bedside table. A faint hum sounded in the distance, and she wondered if it was the generator for the electricity. Tomorrow she'd find out. And explore the place, inside and out.

She was almost asleep when she heard water running in the bathroom and, briefly opening her eyes, saw a thin sliver of light under the door. Minutes later the other door closed.

Soon afterwards she drifted off.

The next morning she slept in, and when she dressed and ventured out of her room the house was quiet, but a yeasty smell led her to the kitchen.

Winnie was standing over a sink, paring some yellow fruit. The woman turned at her entrance, and hastily put down the knife, dropping the peeled fruit into a bowl with some others. 'Morning, Mrs Branson. You want breakfast?'

'There's no hurry,' Stefanie assured her. 'Finish what you're doing. What are those?' She walked over to peer into the bowl.

'Pawpaws. Too many in the garden—I'm pickling them.'

The firm golden globes were bigger than the pawpaws she'd seen in the fruit shops back home, and looked luscious. 'Could I have one for my breakfast?'

'Okay.' Despite Stefanie's instruction, Winnie was washing her hands and snatching a towel from a hook on the wall to dry them. She scooped out one of the slippery fruit with a spoon, opened a cupboard for a plate and deftly sliced the pawpaw, then placed a halved lime on the side, and added a shining spoon and fork from a drawer. 'I'll take it into the dining room for you.'

'No, please.' Stefanie held out her hand and Winnie reluctantly handed her the plate. 'Has Qui—has my husband left?'

'Oh, yes, a while back.'

'Then…' Stefanie looked at the scrubbed wooden table in the centre of the room, with high-backed carved wooden chairs flanking it '…if you don't mind I'll have this here. Then I can talk to you.'

Winnie looked surprised. 'Okay,' she said uncertainly. 'You want anything else? Toast? Juice? Coffee?'

'Coffee would be nice. Why don't you have a cup yourself, and sit down with me?'

The coffee was ready by the time she had finished the pawpaw, and the housekeeper took one of the chairs. When they'd had a second cup she was beginning to relax, readily answering Stefanie's questions about the house and the island.

'Does everyone on Busiata speak English?' Stefanie asked. All the people she'd met so far had been very fluent, with an attractive difference that was more a matter of fully rounded vowels than a definite accent.

'Some of the old people only know Busiatan. But everyone learns English in our schools. It's good, because lots of Busiatans go to Australia or New Zealand for work or education. There's no university on the island, or technical college. And not enough jobs.'

Later Stefanie toured the house, declining Winnie's offer to show her around but avoiding the door that led to Winnie and Roari's quarters in a separate wing, distanced from the house by a short covered walkway.

A large, high-ceilinged lounge faced the driveway, and the dining room opened to a long, narrow glassed-in room shaded by the overhanging roof, furnished with cushioned cane chairs, a glass-topped table, and potplants. The big insect-screened windows had all been thrown open to the air, and the view downhill across dense tropical vegetation allowed a distant glimpse of an unbelievably blue, crushed-chiffon sea spangled with sunlight.

A faint smell of furniture polish pervaded the house, and there wasn't a speck of dust.

The garden was equally well cared for, with not a sign of caterpillar attacks on the glossy shrubs, and scarcely a dead flower.

When she couldn't put it off any longer, she sat down in the airy garden room to write to her family. It wasn't easy, but after several attempts she had two pages that she hoped looked convincing without telling outright lies.

Quinn came home at lunchtime, driven in a sleek dark blue sedan by a uniformed islander. Winnie had set the table on the terrace, and served a ham salad accompanied by thick slices of fresh home-made bread and a jug of iced water.

'How was your morning?' Stefanie asked, watching Quinn spread a dewy butter curl over his bread.

His eyes gleamed with humour as he glanced up at her. 'A very wifely question.' He put down his knife. 'The equipment I asked for has arrived, and later this week I'll be interviewing a short list of candidates for staffing of the computer centre.'

'I'm going to need something to do,' Stefanie said. 'Winnie has the house all under control, and there's nary a weed in the garden.'

'You're not bored already?'

'Of course not—it's all new, and I haven't even explored any of the island yet. But I can't sit about admiring the view and waiting for the next meal for half a year!'

'You'll find something.' He picked up a fork and turned his attention to the meal. 'Don't sweat it.'

All very well for him, Stefanie thought. He had a real job to do and knew how to go about it. She picked up her own fork and viciously speared a tiny tomato, spurting juice onto her dress—just over the centre of her left breast. 'Damn!'

Quinn looked up as she dipped her napkin into the iced water and rubbed at the stain. 'You okay?'

'Yes.' Her voice was crisp. She crumpled the napkin and dropped it onto the table.

'It's a pretty dress. Suits you.' His gaze idly ran over her, lingering on the spot that was now wet and cold. She saw his eyes darken, his lashes flicker, and looked down at herself, flushing as she saw the effect the icy water had produced, her erect nipple clearly visible through the wet fabric.

Hastily she pushed back her chair. 'I'll go and change.'

She ran upstairs, flung off the dress and stuffed it into the clothes basket in the bathroom along with her damp bra, and put on a fresh one and a baggy T-shirt with light cotton trousers.

When she returned to the terrace, her cheeks still

flushed from her haste, Quinn had finished his salad and was leaning against one of the white supporting posts of the pergola, a glass of water in his hand. As she sat down again he said quietly, 'I'm sorry, Stefanie.'

'It's all right.' She picked up her fork, not looking at him. 'I should have thought. I didn't realise…'

He came and resumed his seat opposite her. 'Maybe we should talk about this. I can't promise the same sort of thing won't happen again. It was a natural, instinctive male reaction.' He paused. 'I *can* promise I won't act on those inconvenient impulses.'

'I know you won't.' It was only a short time since Noelle had dumped him, and presumably he was still in love with her. And she was sure he wasn't a man who would force sex on a woman, quite aside from the fact that he needed her here and wouldn't want to frighten her away.

Not that she'd been frightened by the unmistakable sexuality of his riveted gaze. In fact she'd felt a bewilderingly powerful reaction of her own, a surge of answering attraction. It was her shock at that, as much as embarrassment at her predicament, that had sent her fleeing from him.

Pure sex, chemistry, or whatever you wanted to call it, caused surely by the unnatural situation they had put themselves into. Certainly it could have nothing to do with love—both of them were still licking wounds from their previous disastrous relationships.

It was a startling complication. Surely she should have been dead to this kind of feeling for some time. Instead it seemed stronger even than with Bryan. And given the circumstances, that could be risky. As Quinn had warned her, any woman who wanted more from him than he'd offered her was running the risk of getting hurt.

And Stefanie had enough acquaintance with hurt at the moment not to go courting it again.

'I'm glad you trust me,' Quinn said. 'And believe me, I have the greatest respect for you, Stefanie. The last thing I want is to offend you.'

'I told you, it's all right,' she assured him. 'I'm not offended.'

She couldn't tell him she'd actually *liked* it.

The car called for Quinn again, and he said, 'We could drop you off in Iriata if you want to have a look around the town. Later I'll teach you to ride a scooter.'

She spent a couple of hours exploring the little capital. There were two banks, a post office, several general stores and a huge supermarket, plus a number of shops selling colourful tie-dyed and screen-printed sarongs, and nearly all of them displayed linen featuring the appliquéd embroidery that she'd seen on the bedspreads in the house.

When she finally made her way to the pink-painted office building Quinn had pointed out to her she was carrying a long parcel and another, smaller one.

A pleasantly efficient dark-haired young woman ushered her to a big room where Quinn was setting up a bank of computers on a long bench.

'Been shopping?' he enquired, glancing at her.

'I found a great little place run by a woman who took a design course in New Zealand.'

'Uh-huh.' Quinn picked up another cable and undid the wire twist fastening the coils together.

'She's set up an export business in Busiatan craft, specialising in appliqué.'

'It's a tradition here. A lot of it about.'

'Yes, in pastels and floral designs, but she's encouraging the women to branch out into more modern designs. They sell quite well in Australia and New Zealand, apparently, and now she's marketing in Japan.'

'Good for her.' Quinn screwed a fitting into the back of a machine and straightened, smiling at her. 'So what did you buy?'

Stefanie unwrapped the parcel, displaying the wall hanging she'd bought, appliquéd with a swirling abstract design in vivid greens and blues with flashes of silver and a narrow curved strip of pure white.

'I thought it might go in that sunroom at the front of the house.' She spread out the hanging, squinting down at it. 'It sort of reflects the view of the bush and the sea. Do you like it?'

He straightened to look at it. 'Very much. You have good taste. What's in the other parcel, or is it private?'

'Not really.' She unwrapped the colourful tie-dyed sarong, instinctively holding it against her as she had in the shop, stretching the material across the top of her bust. 'What do you think?'

His eyes looked hooded. 'I think,' he drawled, 'it suits you very nicely.'

Abruptly, he turned to unravel another cable.

Flushing, Stefanie dropped the sarong and bundled both purchases up. 'Can I do anything to help?' she asked as she turned, hoping the colour had faded from her cheeks.

'I'm nearly done.' His voice was muffled as he

peered at the back of another machine. 'If you wait a while I'll get the driver to take us home.'

When they got back to the house Winnie handed her a large cream envelope. 'A message from the palace.'

It must have been hand-delivered—the front bore nothing but 'Mr and Mrs Q. Branson' in flowing copperplate lettering.

'Open it,' Quinn said.

She lifted the lightly closed flap and drew out a thick sheet of cream paper. 'We're invited to dinner at the palace,' she told him. 'Tonight at eight o'clock. Do we need to reply?'

'No, it's a royal command, so they'll just expect us. But there's plenty of time for that scooter lesson.'

He'd been right about there being scooters in the garage. Quinn wheeled out one and showed Stefanie how the controls worked. 'It's pretty simple, really. If you hop on I'll ride pillion and help you out.'

He held the machine while she settled herself, then climbed on behind her.

She could feel him at her back, his chest warm and solid, and he leaned forward, his hands over hers, his breath stirring her hair against her cheek as he took her through the starting procedure. 'And to accelerate or slow down just roll your hands gently back or forward on the handles.'

'Okay.' Following his succinct instructions, she brought the engine to life, then started off in rather wobbly fashion down the drive. His hands moved over hers, easing up the speed and straightening the wheel.

'It seems back to front,' she complained breathlessly. 'I'd have thought forward would make it go faster.'

'You'll get used to it.' His cheek brushed hers, slightly raspy but not unpleasant. 'We'll slow down and turn at the gate, onto the lawn.'

As they swung onto the grass he removed his hands from hers to rest them on her waist. 'You're doing great,' he encouraged her. 'Try a circle back to the driveway.'

After half an hour he said, 'Okay, that's enough for the first lesson. Drive it to the garage and stop.'

When they climbed off she looked up at him. 'Thanks. You're a good teacher.'

'I told you it's simple. Next time we'll take it out on the road. Slowly, though.' He reached out and brushed a wayward strand of hair from her face, his warm fingers lightly touching her cheek as he tucked the strand behind her ear. 'You're a quick learner.'

Stefanie stepped back, a strange fluttering feeling in her stomach. 'We'd better get ready for this palace dinner. Will it be very formal?'

'Not nervous, are you?'

'I suppose I am a bit.'

'You'll be fine.' He casually hung his arm about her as they left the garage, his hand cupping her shoulder. 'Just be yourself.'

Still, she took some care over her appearance, washing and drying her hair, then pinning it up with an imitation tortoiseshell comb, and draping a fine gold mesh scarf about the neckline of the apricot dress she'd worn for the wedding ceremony. Slipping a thin gold bangle onto her left wrist, she noticed the gleaming plain band that Quinn had put on her finger only yesterday. Already she'd become used to it.

There was no need for a jacket here. The evening air was still warm, just a little less humid than in the daytime. She had put on pantihose because she was afraid bare legs might not be approved of in palace circles, but the clinging nylon felt rather stifling.

Quinn knocked on the bathroom door and she called, 'Come in.'

He was wearing a lightweight tuxedo with dark pants, and a bow tie. He looked magnificent, virile and confident, and she felt something that was almost like pride. This, she realised again with a small shock, was her husband—albeit temporarily and in name only.

'All ready?' he asked her.

'Yes.' She picked up a small evening bag, and Quinn opened the door for her. On the stairs he took her hand and tucked it into the crook of his arm, closing his warm fingers over hers.

Just inside the big carved door, the man who had driven them from the airport waited, his peaked cap held in big brown hands. The prince must have sent his own car for them.

'Nice to see you again, Tipa,' Stefanie greeted him.

He smiled at her. 'You're looking great tonight, Mrs Branson. *Bakarebu.*'

'*Bakarebu?*'

'Beautiful.'

She laughed. '*Binaka,* Tipa.' She'd learned the Busiatan word for 'thank you' from the housekeeper.

When they were in the car Quinn turned to her. 'Tipa's right, you do look beautiful. I should have told you before.'

She shook her head. 'There's no need.' She knew she looked good, but she'd never been the head-turner that Noelle was. A sudden clutch of sadness squeezed her heart, and she turned away, embarrassed by stupid tears pricking at her eyes.

Quinn's hand closed over hers. 'What is it?'

She blinked rapidly. 'Nothing.' She turned a smile on him. 'I'm fine.'

He leaned closer, searching her face. The interior of the car was dim and she hoped he couldn't see her clearly. But he said, 'You're crying.' He must have seen the sheen of tears in her eyes. His fingers tightened. He lifted his other hand and his thumb wiped a tiny drop of moisture from her cheekbone. Under his breath he said something fierce. 'Bryan?'

Her voice trembled. 'Noelle, actually. Just everything, I guess.'

'If you don't feel up to this tonight I'll tell the driver to take us back.'

'We can't run out on a royal dinner!'

'I'll say you were taken ill.'

'No, I'm all right. Honestly.'

'Sure?'

'I was just being silly. It's over now.'

Unexpectedly he raised her hand to his lips and pressed a brief kiss on it. 'You're not silly.' His voice deepened. 'You're very brave and rather gallant.'

Touched by the gesture, she could almost have cried again. But then the car swept through an imposing pillared gateway where uniformed soldiers stood guard, and up a long, broad driveway to a sprawling two-storied building bathed in floodlights.

As palaces went it was of modest proportions, but for Busiata it was certainly impressive, with its national flag fluttering proudly from a pole at the top of a square turret.

Quinn escorted her up stone steps to wide-flung doors of beaten brass, flanked by more guards, and he paused to show their invitation to the statuesque personage hovering at the entrance.

A young woman, dressed in a narrow ankle-brushing island-print skirt under a long-sleeved white tunic decorated with lace edgings, led them to a reception lounge, lavishly decorated with woven hangings and elaborate carved panels. The king and his family sat in a semi-circle of huge carved chairs. One of the men got up and came to meet them, and Quinn introduced Stefanie to him. 'This is Prince Tuisani.'

'I'm so pleased to meet you, Mrs Branson.' The prince was a big man with a friendly smile. 'And may I offer my congratulations on your recent marriage. I wish you both every happiness.'

Feeling hypocritical, Stefanie returned the smile and the handshake he offered, murmuring, 'Thank you very much.'

'Come,' he said, 'my parents are waiting to meet you.'

The king greeted Quinn like an old friend, heartily shaking his hand, and the queen was gracious to Stefanie, both of them offering further congratulations. Then another lot of guests arrived, and the prince procured glasses of chilled fruit juice for Quinn and Stefanie from one of the circulating waiters, and resumed his seat.

Dinner was served at a long table, with the royals seated at another that formed the top of a T. Stefanie had Quinn on one side and a talkative young Busiatan man on the other. Bright and handsome and not unaware of it, he said he was in the civil service, without explaining exactly what he did.

Course after course was served, and at Quinn's whispered suggestion Stefanie merely tasted each dish. 'There's a lot more to come,' he told her quietly, and she guessed it might give offence if she refused one.

The young man at her other side explained to her some of the less familiar ingredients, queried her extensively about her background, and recounted several humorous incidents from his days at university in New Zealand. Once or twice Stefanie laughed aloud.

His brown eyes dancing, he grinned back at her and insisted, 'It's true! It's all true! You must believe me.'

When they rose from the table Quinn pulled back her chair and then closed his hand about hers. 'You seem to be enjoying yourself.'

'I am, actually.'

He leaned closer, murmuring, 'Remember we're supposed to be newly-weds, and presumably still in the honeymoon stage...*darling*.'

He straightened on the last, slightly louder word as the Crown Prince approached.

'Mrs Branson,' Prince Tuisani said, beaming at her. 'Quinn tells me you are a librarian and that you would be interested in our collection of historical documents.'

'I would love to see them.'

'My father has given permission for you to visit our palace library. I'm afraid you will find the archives in not very good order. Perhaps you might be able to advise us. I believe we have need of some better organisation of our records.'

'I would be delighted,' Stefanie agreed eagerly. 'I

was telling...my husband, I need some kind of occupation.'

'Good. Will tomorrow be suitable? I can send a car for you. Perhaps after one o'clock?'

'Thank you very much. I hope I can help.'

'Thank *you*. Now please excuse me, I must speak to some of our other guests.'

'You've passed muster,' Quinn told her. 'They must have liked you. Not that I'm surprised.' He placed a proprietorial hand on her waist. 'Come over here and I'll introduce you to some more people.'

She met another civil servant and his wife, a member of parliament, and a visiting Australian diplomat, and later chatted for a while with one of the tall, full-figured princesses, briefly wondering if she was the one who had been involved in the coffee-planter scandal, the reason the Busiatans had insisted Quinn be married.

Like many of her countrywomen, the princess had been educated abroad. 'It's good for us to see the world,' she told Stefanie, 'but it's unfortunate that so many of our young people don't want to come back.'

'Did you?' Stefanie asked curiously.

'I knew I must. But I like to fly to Suva sometimes, or Auckland or Sydney, do a bit of shopping and go to a concert or something. Then after a week or two I'm ready to come home. It's more peaceful here. I hope you won't find it too quiet.'

'I'm sure I won't. I come from a small town and it isn't so different, except that Busiata is prettier.'

In the back of the limousine on the way home Stefanie said, 'The royal family are rather nice, aren't they?'

'Yes. Maintaining that balance between dignity and friendliness is quite an art.'

'Most of the islanders seem naturally friendly. I like them.'

'They like you too. Especially your friend at the dinner table.'

Stefanie laughed. 'He was fun. I'm sorry if you felt neglected, but he really hardly stopped talking.'

'He certainly monopolised you. As a new bride I'd have thought you'd be engrossed in your husband,' Quinn said. He sounded almost disapproving.

'But I'm not real—'

Before she could finish the sentence Quinn's head blotted out the moonlight outside the car, and his mouth closed over her astonished lips while his hands gripped her shoulders.

CHAPTER SIX

STEFANIE'S heart lurched in her breast and her blood sizzled.

The kiss lasted only a second, and then Quinn was whispering in her ear, 'We're not alone, remember.'

He drew away, and she looked at the back of Tipa's head and nodded, swallowing. 'Sorry,' she murmured.

When they got out he led her up the steps to the house, an arm about her waist. He'd told Winnie not to wait up, and the door had been left unlatched. Apparently there was no need to lock up on Busiata.

He dropped his arm and closed the door behind them.

'I'm sorry,' she repeated. 'I'll try to watch what I say in future.'

'Right.' He sounded crisp, curt. 'We both should. I'm going to have a nightcap.' No alcohol had been served at the palace. The royal family, she'd gathered, was strictly teetotal. 'Do you want anything?'

'No, thanks.' She felt slightly chilled at his polite but distant manner. 'I think I'll go straight to bed.'

'Goodnight, then.' He waited while she ascended the stairs, making her self-conscious as she felt his steady gaze. At the top she turned, and he was still watching, an enigmatic expression on his granite-carved features. He lifted a hand, and then walked towards the dining room.

When Quinn arrived for lunch the following day Stefanie was in the garden room, standing on a chair

while she hung the appliqué she'd bought the day
before. She saw the car arrive, but didn't hear Quinn
as he came into the room, and when he spoke she
jumped, dropping the wall hanging.

In one stride he was beside her, his hands on her
waist, steadying her. 'I didn't mean to startle you. I
was only saying hello.'

She looked down at him from her perch on the
chair. 'It's okay. Just pass me the hanging, would
you?'

He didn't move immediately, and the warmth of
his hands seeped through her thin T-shirt to her skin.

'I'll do it,' he said. His grip tightened and she instinctively clutched his shoulders as he lifted her
down.

For a moment longer he held her, only inches sep-
arating them, his eyes holding hers with a long, unreadable look. Then her hands slid from his shoulders
and he released her, turning to pick up the hanging.
He didn't even need the chair to reach the hook she
had put in place.

After lunch the prince's car called for Stefanie and
took her to the palace, where she was met by the
prince himself and escorted to the library. It was a
huge room where books both old and relatively new
were lined along deep shelves with little sign of logical order. The archives were housed in an attic room
above it, and consisted of shelves and cupboards
crammed with books, folders, envelopes and boxes.
Some looked as though they had been gathering dust
for fifty years or more. Rolled maps and charts and
old paintings stood in corners or leaned against the

shelves, and the long, low-ceilinged space was un-
bearably hot.

'It would take weeks just to see what's there,'
Stefanie told Quinn that evening as they sat with their
after-dinner coffee in the glassed-in room, while a
huge coppery moon rose rapidly from the darkened
sea. 'And no one could work in that stuffy attic.
Everything will have to be carried down to the library
for sorting.'

'Not by you,' Quinn said.

He wasn't laying down the law to her, was he? Her
head lifted. 'I'd like to help sort the archives. I've
already told the prince I'm willing.'

'If you want to do it, fine. But they'll have to find
someone else for the heavy work.'

'How am I supposed to tell them that?'

'If you don't, I will.'

Stefanie gave a little laugh. 'That sounds awfully
like a husband.'

Quinn gave her a glinting smile. 'That's what I am,
and don't forget it.'

Absurdly, Stefanie's heart seemed to skip a couple
of beats. She put her coffee cup back in the saucer
and said dulcetly, 'Your word is my command, O lord
and master.'

It was his turn to laugh. 'I wish you meant that.'

'Is that the kind of wife you really want?' Bite your
tongue, she scolded herself. The wife he really wanted
was Noelle, you fool.

Quinn shook his head. 'I'm very satisfied for the
moment with the wife I have. I couldn't have made
a better choice.'

For the moment. Well, he'd said she was ideal for
the part he'd asked her to play, and he still thought

so. She should have been pleased. Instead she felt inexplicably annoyed. 'You sound very smug,' she told him.

'I meant it as a compliment.'

Which was how she should have taken it. Probably it was the heat that was making her unusually touchy and faintly irritable.

And of course there was the constant, nagging ache of Bryan's defection, always there in the background. Or nearly always. But at times she'd almost forgotten the hard, heavy weight inside her.

'I don't mean to bully you,' Quinn said. 'But I brought you here and I feel responsible. It's only fair that I take care of your comfort, and I won't allow you to be exploited or overworked. I don't want you to regret…anything.'

'I'm responsible for myself, Quinn.' But she kept her voice mild, not wanting to start a quarrel. Making an effort to relax, she added, 'I think I'm going to like it here. Already I feel better about…things. I suppose it's being away from everything familiar, anything that might remind me…'

'I'm glad. I'm finding it easier too. You're a very restful person to be with, Stefanie.'

She supposed that was a compliment too. It didn't necessarily mean unexciting, she scolded herself. But she doubted he'd found Noelle restful. Stimulating, maybe. She sighed soundlessly.

They were silent for a while, watching the moon grow smaller and paler as it climbed up the sky. Stars spread across the velvety expanse, coldly glittering.

'How are the interviews going?' Stefanie asked. He had started seeing prospective job candidates.

'They're all dead keen but none of them are properly qualified. There hasn't been much work for computer technicians on Busiata until now.'

'It will change the island, won't it, this scheme?'

'Even a place as remote as this can't just opt out of the world economy these days. At least they're taking charge of their own destiny.'

'I guess that's important.'

'They're very proud that Busiata was never colonised. It's quite an achievement for a tiny nation state.'

A few days later Prince Tui, as he invited her to call him, formally requested Stefanie's help in cataloguing the archives, offering a modest wage. She accepted, glad that while she was here she could be financially independent of Quinn without depleting her savings after all.

Two burly members of the palace guard carried all the archives down from the attic, lining them up on the library floor in neat rows, and every weekday Tipa called for Stefanie in the prince's limousine.

After a few more lessons on the scooter she was given her licence, but the prince insisted she continue to use the transport he provided. Remembering what Quinn had told her about the employment problem, she supposed there wasn't enough otherwise for the chauffeur to do.

She and Quinn breakfasted together, and were driven home for lunch and again in time for dinner. A car would be waiting for her at five, but Quinn usually arrived home somewhat later than she did. They got into the habit of having a short swim in their private pool before lunch and dinner. Quinn swam a dozen lengths with long, purposeful overarm strokes while Stefanie gently breast-stroked or floated on her back.

One day she was tucking a towel about herself sarong-fashion when Quinn heaved himself out of the pool, his shoulders flexing. He straightened and strolled over to where he'd dropped his towel on the tiles. Swinging round as he lifted it, he caught her gaze on him.

She'd been admiring the lithe masculinity of his body, the taut haunches and strong thighs that streamed with water—staring, she realised as he raised his brows enquiringly.

He stood with the towel in his hands, and his mouth quirked as he returned the stare, his eyes turning a deeper green when his gaze slipped down her bare legs and up again over her towel-wrapped body.

Hastily Stefanie turned away, going to the house to change. Stupid to have looked at him that way, except that any normal woman would have noticed that Quinn looked awfully good wearing only swim briefs.

They'd been two weeks on the island when Quinn suggested that on Saturday they might ride higher into the hills on the scooters, and explore. 'We could pack a picnic,' he suggested. 'Or ask Winnie to make us one. It should be cooler up there, and there's a waterfall if we can find it, so bring your swimsuit.'

They found the waterfall, after bumping over increasingly rough and narrow roads until the scooters were slowed to snail pace. Eventually they abandoned them when the road became no more than a narrow track among enormous yellow-flowered hibiscus and ragged-leaved banana trees with spectacular blood-red blooms.

The early part of the journey had taken them past houses where children stared and giggled and called *'Sambuda!'* and adults straightened from working in their taro patches to wave.

Now all signs of habitation had been left behind, and the only sound was the rustle of a mountain breeze in the bushes and the occasional plop of a hibiscus blossom falling on the damp path.

Quinn had stuffed their things into a canvas pack and was leading the way, sweeping overhanging branches aside and holding them for Stefanie.

The path became steeper and she stopped, panting. 'Are you sure about this waterfall?'

'It's on the map,' he told her. 'Look.' He pulled the folded chart from his pocket.

She regarded the dotted line that was presumably the track, eventually stopping at a wavy blue line and a very long Busiatan word with the English words beside it: 'Bridal Veil Waterfall'.

'Original,' she remarked dryly. 'There are at least two falls with the same name back home in New Zealand.'

'I don't suppose it's a translation of the Busiatan name. If that has anything to do with brides—' He stopped there and shot her a glance before stuffing the map back into his pocket. 'We should be nearly there. In fact, I think I can hear it. Isn't that the sound of water?'

Stefanie listened intently. A bird was calling some-where distantly—a fluting two notes, repeated. And yes, there was a faint sound of rushing water. 'All right,' she said. 'After you, Macduff.'

'There's no hurry. Have I been going too fast for you?'

'No, not at all. If there's cool water around here, I want to get to it— *Oh!*' She jumped and instinctively moved closer to him.

Automatically he put a steadying arm about her shoulders. 'What is it?'

'Something just whipped into the bushes over there. It looked horribly like a snake.'

'There aren't any on Busiata.'

'Are you sure?'

'According to my information. New Zealand isn't the only place in the world that doesn't have them. It's probably a lizard.'

'An awfully big one!'

'I believe they can be quite large. But they're harmless.'

She had seen lizards in the garden—small, darting iridescent blue creatures with gleaming black eyes, and bigger green ones that crawled up the outer walls of the house, blinking in the sun.

'A lizard, you reckon?' she queried, easing from his hold, although she'd been grateful for the solid feel of his male bulk and the strong fingers curling about her shoulder.

'There aren't too many nasties here. A couple of biting spiders, and round the reef you have to watch for spiny things, I'm told. But apart from that, as I said, it's pretty close to Paradise.'

'Okay.' She cast a wary glance at the spot where she'd seen the creature, and sidled past. 'I believe you.'

'I won't let you walk into any danger, Stefanie,' he assured her.

'Thanks, Tarzan,' she muttered, and heard him laugh softly.

The waterfall, when they found it, was worth the trek. It spilled from a mossy cleft at the top of a bluff, spreading in foamy white droplets that seemed airily suspended before plunging into a natural rock basin, wet mosses and ferns trembling and dripping on the cliff beside it.

A fallen tree trunk lying on the ground made a natural seat for Stefanie and Quinn to have their picnic lunch. They were packing away the remains when a party of teenagers and younger children burst from the path and greeted them with shy smiles before the boys stripped off their T-shirts and the girls their dresses, and they plunged into the pool wearing shorts, slips or bathing suits.

While Stefanie and Quinn watched they played about, splashing, swimming fish-like underwater, the older ones daring each other to climb the cliff and dive from rocky outcrops.

A little girl wearing a soaked white slip came out of the water and stood staring at the strangers, a forefinger hooked into her mouth.

'*Sambuda,*' Stefanie said. 'What's your name?'

The child giggled and looked down at her bare toes, then whispered, 'Siona.'

'Siona? That's pretty.'

The girl giggled again, and came a bit closer. 'You a pretty lady,' she said.

'Thank you. How old are you, Siona?'

'Um...four years. Soon I'm going to school.'

'Siona!' one of the older boys called, and she turned. The boy said something rapidly in Busiatan, and she replied.

'Is that your brother?' Stefanie asked her.

Siona nodded. 'He say don't bother you.'

'It's all right.' Turning to the boy, Stefanie told him, 'It's all right. She's not bothering us.'

By the time the others came out of the water and were getting ready to go, Siona was sitting between Stefanie and Quinn, happily chatting.

After they had all left Quinn said, 'You like kids, do you?'

'Mostly. Don't you?'

'I guess so. She seemed a particularly charming child. Did you and Bryan plan to have a family?'

'I think we both took that for granted. Didn't you and Noelle?'

He didn't answer for a moment. 'I suppose I was taking it for granted too. I'm not sure how Noelle felt about anything, now.'

She knew what he meant. You thought you knew a person, and then found that they had a secret life you knew nothing about. So who were you to judge anyone else's feelings?

Quinn stood up. 'Want me to turn my back while you get your swimsuit on?'

'I'm wearing it.' She started to take off her shorts and T-shirt.

'Me too.' He quickly stripped, and was in the pool before her.

When she followed the water felt cold, but she soon adjusted to the temperature, stroking in leisurely fashion towards the waterfall, keeping to its outskirts. After a while she got out and laid her towel on the mossy ground, stretching out on her front to allow the sun that struck through the space above the pool to dry her.

Shortly afterwards Quinn joined her, lying on his

back, and they stayed there without speaking for some time.

Almost asleep, Stefanie twisted and sat up, not wanting to doze off and get burnt. She flung back her damp hair and contemplated the waterfall, mesmerised by its constant yet ever-changing movement.

Quinn shifted to pillow his head on his hands, and murmured, 'I must say, it's a perfect spot for a honeymoon.'

'Yes.' And without warning her eyes filled with hot tears, burning down her cheeks before she could hide them.

'Damn!' Quinn jerked upright beside her. 'That was a stupid thing to say...'

She lifted a hand to wipe at the tears, her throat closing on a choked sob. And his arms came about her, pulling her to his warm, bare chest, his hands stroking her arms and shoulders.

She stiffened momentarily, shocked at her loss of control, bewildered by the unexpected flood of grief. But he didn't allow her to pull away, his cheek brushing her temple as he held her close. 'Let it go,' he said quietly. 'It's time.'

The storm of weeping washed over her, and she slumped into his firm embrace and let him comfort her, glad of the strong arms cradling her until the sobs gradually abated and she was resting, exhausted, against him. 'Sorry,' she said, her voice muffled.

'No need. It had to come eventually.'

'Did it come to you?' she asked him, doubting it.

'Not exactly the same way. I got a bottle of whisky one night and drank myself into a state of forgetfulness. Something I've never done before, and an experience I wouldn't want to repeat. But I suppose it had much the same effect.'

She picked up a corner of the crumpled towel and wiped her nose, easing away from him. 'I must look a sight.'

His arms still loosely holding her, Quinn smiled. 'No.' He smoothed a tangled skein of her hair back from her hot face. 'A bit pink and pathetic.'

Pathetic. Stefanie grimaced.

Quinn's smile turned to a crooked little grin. He dipped his head and kissed her nose. His lips wandered to her cheek. He drew back a fraction, and his eyes changed, darkened—and with infinite, breath-stopping slowness, he lowered his head again until his mouth touched her swollen, trembling one.

She felt drained and listless, but Quinn's mouth moving gently, persuasively on hers brought warmth and life seeping back into her soul. Tentatively she responded, and his kiss became firmer, parting her throbbing lips.

Time spun away, and the trees around them seemed to recede, the sound of the waterfall becoming a distant hush. She could feel the texture of Quinn's bare skin where her palm rested on his chest. His hand smoothed her back, then shaped the inward curve of her waist, and finally found the soft mound of her breast.

Her heartbeat accelerated, and she felt his hand tighten, knew that he could feel her reaction, even before his thumb flicked over the hardened centre of her breast, scarcely shielded by the damp satin of her swimsuit.

Stefanie made a small sound in her throat, and he

shifted his position, gently bore her back to the soft, cushiony moss, and made her mouth open for him.

Her hands moved over his chest to his shoulders, finally sliding behind his neck, her arms clinging. His body was warm and heavy, his legs muscular and tantalisingly rough against her thighs, and she could feel his burgeoning arousal.

Sensation washed over her, sweeping away thought, sense, memory. All that mattered was this burning, consuming physical need. A need she instinctively knew that Quinn could satisfy. She didn't want to think any more, just plunge into this dizzying maelstrom, let herself be swept away by the things his mouth, his hands, his eager male body were doing to her.

He slipped the strap of her swimsuit from her shoulder, and lifted his head, pushed down the material further and looked at her, her bare breast now cupped in his big hand.

Then his glittering gaze moved to her face, her half-closed eyes and parted, kiss-warmed lips. 'Stefanie...' he said hoarsely. She saw him swallow, and his jaw went taut as he looked at her. He said something under his breath, and then his hand left her skin, pulled up the strap back onto her shoulder. He closed his eyes momentarily, giving his head a little shake.

And then he was rolling away, sitting up, rubbing a fist across his forehead as he bent his head, saying as if the word was wrenched from between his teeth, 'Sorry.'

Stefanie struggled up too, drawing her knees into encircling arms, trying not to shiver despite the sun's warmth. 'Sorry?' She hadn't exactly fought him off.

The whole thing—such as it was—had been totally mutual.

Quinn lifted his head, meeting her dazed eyes with a banked green fire in his. He said huskily, 'I didn't intend to do that. It wasn't supposed to happen.'

Stefanie licked her lips. What had just happened here? 'Because we're not supposed to be...'

'Lovers?' he suggested as she hesitated. 'That's right, we're only supposed to be married.' His mouth twisted. 'Ironic, isn't it?' Thrusting a hand over his hair, he said again, 'Sorry.'

'It's as much my fault as yours.' She'd been nestling in his arms with practically nothing on, and she certainly hadn't objected when he'd started to kiss her.

'It was unfair. You were feeling vulnerable and I took advantage.' He stood up, hauling on his shirt, and turned to pull on his shorts. 'You didn't know what you were doing.'

Had he?

Slowly she got up too, reached for her own clothes and put them on, still feeling disoriented and very confused. How could she have gone so quickly from crying her eyes out over Bryan to passionately kissing Quinn? *Wanting* Quinn? She'd never been the kind of girl who went easily from one love affair to another. In fact the only man she'd been seriously involved with had been Bryan, after a few innocent experimental relationships.

She'd thought their marriage would have a solid basis because they'd known each other so long and love had crept up on them rather than arriving in a blinding flash. Yet it had all been an illusion.

And maybe this was too. Quinn was right, of

course; neither of them was ready to embark on an affair only weeks after being jilted, and she should be glad he'd called a halt.

Quinn picked up the pack and slung it to his shoulder. 'Coming?'

She followed him back along the track to the scooters, hardly noticing the leaves that brushed her shoulder, sometimes her cheeks or hair. He seemed preoccupied too, silently checking on her with a brief glance behind, or simply lifting a branch out of her way.

Once they remounted the scooters she was glad of the necessity to concentrate on negotiating the ruts and treacherous tree roots that made the dirt road tricky, until they reached a more populated part of the island and a better surface.

Back at the house, Quinn said he had some work to catch up on, and disappeared into his room.

Stefanie went to her own, and sat on the bed for a long time, trying to work out her muddled feelings, without a great deal of success.

'I was wondering,' she told Quinn at lunch a few days later, 'if you could set up a computer database for me to use in the archiving project. Prince Tui said to ask you.'

'Sure.' He looked up from his salad. 'Do they have a computer there?'

'He said they could bring one from the palace office into the library.'

'How urgent is it? I'm pretty snowed under right now.'

'I know. As soon as you can manage it, though.'

'You'll need to show me exactly what you need. We could have a look tonight.'

The prince sent his car for them after dinner, and when they arrived accompanied them to the library, but after checking that the computer already sitting at one end of the long solid table in the centre of the room was adequate for the job, he left them.

Quinn switched on the machine and pulled two chairs up. 'Tell me what you want.'

'I need to index by subject, date, author—where there is one—and title, and to cross-reference entries.'

'Well, there's a basic database program in here. Let's see if we can set it up to deal with your type of materials.'

Sitting shoulder to shoulder with him, she watched the format take shape on the screen.

For over an hour he refined and customised the system until Stefanie was satisfied. 'Yes,' she said, leaning forward. 'That looks great!'

She turned to him as she sat back again, disconcerted to find him closer than she'd expected, his face only inches from hers.

Abruptly Quinn pushed his chair further from the table—and from hers. 'I'll save it and set up a screen shortcut for you.'

'Thank you.' She suddenly realised how warm the air was, even with a fan twirling overhead. Standing up, she went to the papers she'd laid out on the table during the day, randomly shifting a cardboard folder, only to put it back in exactly the same place.

Quinn said, 'Let's make sure it all works. Do you have something there you want to list?'

Stefanie indicated the dozens of documents, and

picked up a sheaf of yellowing paper. 'This is one of the Reverend Burford's sermons.'

'The old boy himself?' Quinn looked intrigued as he stood up and indicated she should take his chair.

'In his own handwriting,' she confirmed, carefully placing the brittle pages beside the computer.

Quinn closed a hand on the back of the chair, his knuckles briefly brushing her shoulder-blade, and bent forward to peer at the crabbed writing.

She shifted slightly, willing away the tingling sensation from her skin.

'Is it all right to touch?' Quinn asked, ready to lift the page and view the next sheet.

'As long as you treat it very gently.'

'I know how to be gentle,' he promised, turning the paper. After a couple of seconds he laughed softly. 'He seems to have thought Busiata was a den of iniquity.' He glanced at the laden table. 'Are the archives all in English?'

'There are some in Busiatan, although they didn't have a written language before the missionaries came. I'm putting those aside for a translator. Now...I start here?'

Quinn took her patiently through the process, once placing his hand over hers to guide the pointer. His breath stirred a wisp of hair at her temple, and her skin prickled again. She took a quick breath of her own, fixing her gaze on the screen before her so intently that her eyes watered.

Then Quinn straightened and stepped back and to one side, jamming both hands in his pockets.

'Type in your note at the cursor point,' he said, his voice slightly strained.

She hit a wrong key and had to 'Undo' and try again. The next time she got it right.

'Good,' Quinn said coolly. 'You can shut it down now.' He moved away, glancing at the piles of material on the table. 'Is there much more of this stuff?'

'Heaps. I'm not sure if I can finish the job inside six months, but I suppose once the system is in place someone else could take over.'

He picked up a shabby, leather-bound book, anciently stained with sea-water, and she said, 'That's the ship's log from a whaler that foundered on the reef in the 1870s.'

Quinn opened the book, careful to support the spine, and she thought what nice hands he had, remembering how he'd cupped one over her breast at the waterfall while he kissed her. As he'd said, he did know how to be gentle.

She gazed at his bent head while he skimmed a page, apparently absorbed in the words of a long-dead mariner.

'It gives you a strange feeling, doesn't it?' he said, looking across the table at Stefanie.

'It's a thrill, seeing words written by someone who lived so long ago. You'll never meet, and yet you feel in an eerie sort of way that you know them.'

Quinn nodded. 'I "know" people all around the world I'll probably never meet, who I communicate with through the internet. My work establishes connections over space, yours does the same over the boundaries of time.'

'Yes.' Silently she wondered if the two of them would ever feel that connection with each other. They lived side by side, maintaining an invisible wall between them which they were careful not to breach.

Underneath their daily lives Stefanie sensed a tension that she instinctively knew Quinn felt too, like a tightrope stretched between them that neither dared to set foot on, because it was too far from the ground and they couldn't see a safety net.

CHAPTER SEVEN

QUINN worked long hours, sometimes not arriving home until it was time for the evening meal. He moved a desk into his bedroom, and often when she put down her book to go to sleep, Stefanie could see his light was on, reflecting off the bushes outside and attracting insects that whirred and floated in circles and sometimes hurled themselves at the screens.

He came home one day from work to find Stefanie talking to a young Busiatan man in the airy front room. She'd opened the door to him half an hour ago and was leafing through a colourfully jacketed book when Quinn walked in.

She looked up, saw him glance at the jug of cold fruit juice on the table between the two lounging chairs, and raise his brows enquiringly.

The man beside her got to his feet. 'Mr Branson, how do you do? I have been talking to your lovely wife—'

'About what?' Quinn asked sharply, glancing at Stefanie.

'I am a representative of the Scripture Institute of the Pacific. We have a special offer that I've been explaining to Mrs Branson—'

'You're a salesman?'

'We bring the scriptures to the people. The king has endorsed our organisation. This family bible—'

'We don't have a family.'

Stefanie said, 'I already told Mr Harding—'

'Ah—' The man beamed '—but when you are newly married is a good time to buy. Then, when you have your first child—' As he spoke, he picked up the briefcase standing by his chair, starting to rummage inside it.

'We'll wait, thanks,' Quinn said. 'Stefanie—if you've finished with that—?'

Taking the hint, Stefanie closed the book in her lap and handed it back to the salesman. 'Thank you,' she said. 'Maybe another time.'

'I'll leave my card,' he said, looking disappointed.

Quinn said, 'I'll see Mr Harding out.'

When he came back Stefanie had poured herself another drink and one for him. 'You gave him short shrift,' she said.

'I didn't think they had door-to-door sales here.' Quinn dropped into the chair and picked up his glass. 'Why did you let him in?'

'I didn't see any harm. *Do* you own a bible?'

'Doesn't everyone? Do you think you were wise?'

'Wise?' Stefanie looked blankly at him.

With a touch of impatience he said, 'I told you how the Busiatans are about morality between men and women. Having a tête-à-tête with a good-looking young man isn't very discreet behaviour for a newly married woman.'

At his censorious tone Stefanie laughed disbelievingly. 'Have you ever seen a Busiatan under fifty who's *not* good-looking? I only offered him a cold drink while I looked at what he had to offer—and you didn't give me a chance to say if I wanted to buy or not, either.'

Quinn looked at her. 'Did you want to?'

'Probably not. But you took the decision out of my hands.'

'I'd assumed you'd have spoken up if you were interested.'

She probably would have. But she wasn't ready to let the subject go. 'When my husband had just said "No, thanks"? What would the Busiatans make of that? Aren't they into the obedient wives thing?'

'Very likely.' Quinn smiled faintly. 'But you're not?'

'Hardly.'

'That's what I thought. Pity.' He sipped at his drink.

Stefanie gave him an eloquent look.

He returned her a teasing glance. 'You rise beautifully.'

'You asked for it.'

'True. I like seeing you take the bait. Your eyes sparkle and the way you tilt your chin makes me want to—'

'Punch it?' she suggested pugnaciously.

'No.' For an instant his smiling gaze settled on her mouth, and the air stilled.

Then the moment passed and he settled back in his chair. 'I thought inviting salesmen in was the ploy of desperate, lonely housewives.'

'So?' Stefanie parried.

His brows arched. 'You have a job—'

'Yes, but...!'

'But?'

'Oh, nothing,' she muttered discontentedly, picking up her glass.

'Tell me.'

'Why?' she demanded.

Quinn frowned slightly. 'You think I'm not interested? But I am, Stefanie.'

'Really?' Hearing with startled shame the sharpness in her own voice, she immediately backtracked. 'I know you're very busy. It's all right, really. It's not as though—well, as though this is a normal marriage.'

He looked at her carefully. 'Have I made you unhappy, Stefanie?'

'I'm not unhappy. But…do you think we can be friends, not just two people living in the same house?'

'Friends,' he said. 'I thought we were. Or are you saying you want more than that?'

'No,' she denied hastily. 'No.'

He looked away, veiling his eyes. 'I suppose you're feeling neglected—'

'I don't mean that.'

'No, you're right. I promised you a holiday. You're not only working after all, you're bored when you're not, and it's up to me to do something about it. I scolded you for not acting like a newly-wed. Maybe it's time I took my own advice. I'll try to do better.'

'You don't have to keep an eye on me because I'm bored!' She didn't want his grudging company. 'I'm not going to create another coffee-planter scandal in reverse.'

'I wasn't suggesting you would. If you ever do get that bored, I thought I'd made it clear that you needn't look further afield.'

'I'll keep it in mind,' she assured him with deceptive calm. 'But I doubt I'll ever be *that* bored!'

It was a nasty crack, and she was relieved when after a moment he laughed. 'All right, I'll let you have that one. I guess I shouldn't have brought the subject up.'

*   *   *

The following Saturday they took their scooters to one of the island's well-populated coral beaches, and Quinn taught Stefanie to snorkel.

He was patient and thorough and rather aloof, and she couldn't help noticing how scrupulous he was about not touching her unnecessarily when he showed her how to use the mask and breathing tube, or adjusted the fit of her rubber flippers. She couldn't help laughing as they awkwardly approached the water, lifting their webbed flippers to negotiate the soft sand.

Quinn grinned down at her. 'I know, it's ludicrous, but they'll help a lot.'

Then he led her into the lagoon and they explored a silent undersea world of brilliant coral and anemones. Sometimes he touched her arm and pointed to a striped, iridescent fish darting by, or a particularly striking coral formation. His fingers slipped on her wet skin. When he grasped her hand to steer her in another direction, she followed willingly, her fingers curling about his.

When they came out at last, pulling off their masks, Quinn bent to remove her flippers for her. She looked down at his water-sleeked head and resisted an urge to touch him, run her fingers along the gleaming skin of his strong shoulders.

Then he straightened and handed her flippers to her. 'Thank you,' she said. 'I could have managed.'

'Next time. You're still new at this.' He quickly removed his own flippers. Straightening, he hooked an arm loosely about her shoulders, then removed it as though he'd recalled his determination to adopt a hands-off policy. Stefanie felt an unaccountable depression settle around her heart.

Some islanders who had speared fish and crabs and

were cooking them on the sand over a driftwood fire beckoned Stefanie and Quinn over to share their bounty.

The fresh seafood was wonderfully tasty, washed down with milk from coconuts gathered on the spot by children who climbed the tall, skinny palms as easily as they swam in the lagoon.

'Do you spear-fish too?' Stefanie asked Quinn as they returned to the scooters later.

He shook his head. 'Tried it but I seem to have missed out on the hunting, shooting, fishing instinct. I suppose I could do it if I was starving on a desert island or something, but as sport, it didn't interest me. The islanders catch fish for the table, of course, or sell them to make a living.'

'I guess that's different,' Stefanie agreed. She too would be content to explore the inner reef, swimming among striped orange-and-black, butter-yellow and green fish without feeling any urge to kill them.

They got to know their neighbours, and spent pleasant Sunday afternoons lounging on porches or in chairs set under trees, talking to the background strum of a guitar.

Children would come and go, staring shyly or daring to ask questions before darting away to their own pursuits. There was no television station, but a couple of video hire shops in the capital did a thriving trade in action adventure films, old cartoon features and vintage musicals.

'I wonder what kind of picture they're getting of the rest of the world.' Stefanie commented one night.

'A very odd one, I should think,' Quinn answered.

One balmy tropical evening they attended a song-

and-dance fest held in a nearby village. Groups of performers came from miles around, and although no prizes were awarded, dozens of supporters turned up to cheer and clap. Stefanie and Quinn sat among the islanders on the dry ground.

A woman ran forward with a flower and tucked it into a man's skimpy waist-cloth, then retired giggling to sit among her friends. While the women were dancing a man stood up and danced face to face with one of them for a few minutes, coming closer and closer with outstretched arms but never quite touching. When he went back to the crowd another followed, choosing a different woman.

People laughed, and it wasn't hard to guess at the gist of the remarks that were called out, even when they were in Busiatan. Flirting was much the same all over the world.

Watching another of the women's groups perform, Stefanie heard Quinn give a low laugh, and felt the vibration against her shoulder. She turned an enquiring look on him.

He took his eyes from the dancers and brought his mouth closer to her ear to murmur, 'The missionaries did their best to stamp out fornication and debauchery, but they never really managed to turn the islanders into a bunch of puritans, did they?'

Stefanie turned back to the dancers, every one of them wearing a long, all-enveloping dress covering her from neck to ankle, shoulder to wrist. But each woman also had a broad sash tied about her seductively swaying hips. Fluttering hands moved in unison from breast to waist, then lifted into the air as the women boldly smiled and made graceful beckoning gestures.

She sent Quinn a smile of agreement, her eyes meeting his in silent amusement.

Then it was the men's turn again, their dances chest-slapping, knee-lifting, foot-stamping exhibitions of virility. The church-going, Reverend Burford-influenced modern Busiatans might frown on overt sexuality, but their traditional dances and songs told a different story about the past.

The insistent rhythms and uninhibited gestures made Stefanie's blood run faster. She became very conscious of Quinn's shoulder pressed against hers, his strong thigh only inches from her own. She could even feel him breathing. Her whole body began to tingle with warmth, a stirring of excitement.

She tried to blot out the feelings, alarmed at the trend of them. Propinquity, she told herself, that's all it is. An inconvenient and potentially embarrassing sexual attraction. Maybe the well-known rebound syndrome.

Nothing lasting. Nothing deep or meaningful. In other words, not what she wanted at all. And Quinn had warned her that he wasn't looking for anything of the kind.

The dancing over, food was spread out on clean woven mats and Stefanie handed over a box of baked nut squares to be shared, before accepting the invitation to tuck into rice cakes, slices of fresh fruit, and strips of dried fish and salted pork.

Quinn reached up and plucked a scarlet hibiscus from an overhanging branch, and tucked it into the knot of hair that Stefanie had loosely fastened at her nape for coolness.

She blinked at him, and he grinned. 'Practically

every other woman has at least one flower. I was beginning to feel remiss.'

But the light in his eyes was disturbing, and his gaze held hers for a long moment before he looked away, leaving her feeling shaken and more disturbed than ever.

It was dark by the time they made for home in the glow of a huge orange moon. Riding their scooters in and out of the shadows of overhanging palms, they caught occasional glimpses of the night-black lagoon showing glimmers of white where the waves broke over the reef.

On a lonely stretch of road closed in by thick-growing banana palms and the rampant island shrubs, Stefanie's scooter sputtered a couple of times and the motor died.

Quinn did a U-turn and came back to her. 'Trouble?' He killed his own engine.

'It can't be petrol.' She knew he'd checked them both over before they left the house.

'Let's have a look.'

But the motor was unresponsive, no matter what he did. 'We'll leave it and pick it up in the morning,' he said, wheeling the machine to the side of the road. 'Hop on the back of mine and hold on to me.' He was already straddling his machine, waiting for her. She took a deep breath and did as he'd said, winding her arms loosely about his waist.

He started up the motor and took off. A bump in the road startled her and involuntarily she tightened her grip, her breasts pressing against his back.

'Okay?' he asked over his shoulder.

'Yes.' He was very warm and she could smell the clean scent of his skin through his cotton shirt. She was tempted to lay her cheek on his shoulder. Instead she lifted her head, letting the wind created by their movement cool her face and blow her hair back from her forehead. She felt light and free and almost happy, riding through the night with her arms about Quinn's solid waist, her heart thudding quietly against his back.

The road was winding uphill, the scooter headlamp picking out the plants at its edge, and briefly lighting on pale, fluttering moths. Then they were through the gate and sweeping into the open garage.

Stefanie released her hold and got off. 'Thanks.'

The light was doused and Quinn's shadowy bulk appeared beside her. 'No problem—well, none that I can't handle.'

They moved out into the moonlight and she said, 'You think you can fix it tomorrow?'

'I wasn't talking about the scooter, but I suspect that's a fuel blockage.'

'What were you talking about, then?'

Heading rapidly towards the house, he suddenly stopped and looked down at her. 'You.'

'Me?'

He made an impatient gesture. 'Us, then. This situation. When I said I could stand six months of celibacy, I have to admit I hadn't envisaged it would be so hard to keep my word.'

'Oh. I see.' She did see, all too clearly. 'It…isn't that easy for me either,' she confessed.

Quinn drew in a breath. She heard it.

'I guess,' she said hesitantly, 'we're both still…a bit off balance. I mean…we've hardly had time to get over what happened, have we? And we've been thrown into this…'

'Actually I dragged you into it.'

'I had a choice. I could have said no.'

'You can still say no to…anything more I ask of you. Remember that.'

Didn't he trust himself not to make further demands? She thought her heart skipped a beat or two. 'I know that. But you haven't asked.'

There was a tiny silence. In an odd voice he asked, 'Do you want me to?'

'No!' she answered quickly, too quickly. 'It…wouldn't be sensible, would it? There's too much we both need to work through.'

'You're right, of course. Sorry I brought the subject up.'

'Getting it out in the open might help clear the air.'

He turned and started walking again. 'Maybe.'

They were invited to the palace to celebrate the king's birthday at an afternoon function with hundreds of others. The big reception room was thronged with people paying their respects, and the crowd overflowed to the grounds where food and drink were freely available at long tables, each one with a whole roasted pig as a centrepiece.

Nibbling on a piece of fresh pineapple while Quinn was engaged in conversation with a local doctor, Stefanie moved into the shade of a huge breadfruit tree.

'Mrs Branson—nice to meet you again.'

She turned and recognised her talkative table neighbour from the first royal dinner that she and Quinn had attended.

He beamed at her. 'I'm Tembua Tualala. We have met—'

'Yes, I remember. How nice to see you again, Mr Tualala.'

'No, you must call me Tom. That's my New Zealand name.'

'Then I'm Stefanie.'

'How are you liking Busiata, Stefanie?'

'Very much. My husband told me it was the nearest thing to Paradise he'd ever seen, and he was right.'

'Ah, your husband...' Tom looked about. 'I see him.'

Quinn turned his head just then, said something to the man he was with and strode over, his hand closing lightly around Stefanie's arm. 'You okay?'

'Yes. You remember Mr Tualala—Tom? We met at the palace before.'

'I remember.' He gave the other man a nod of acknowledgement before turning back to her. 'Would you like a drink? Iced tea or a fruit juice?'

'Juice would be nice.'

She expected him to leave and fetch it, but instead he said, 'It's over there. Excuse us, won't you?' he added politely to Tom. 'Maybe we'll see you later.'

As he led her away through the crowd Stefanie said uneasily, 'What was that about?'

He looked surprised. 'What?'

'The jealous husband act, dragging me away from him.'

'Dragging you?' His hold on her arm was still light, a mere touch just above her elbow.

'You know what I mean. We were only talking, for heaven's sake! And in full view of half the island's population. No one could have thought I was flirting with the man.'

'Couldn't they?' He slanted her a strange glance.

'If you were enjoying yourself I can only apologise. I thought you found him a bit of a bore at that dinner.'

'He did talk a lot, but he'd scarcely got in two words this time before you were over there looking all proprietorial and dog-in-the-mangerish. I thought any second you might start beating your chest and saying ''This my woman!'''

'And I'd hoped you might be grateful for being rescued. Shall I take you back to him?'

'Of course not. I just thought you were rather fast off the mark.' She recalled him behaving similarly with Noelle, and glanced up at him with wary curiosity, but there was none of the veiled sexuality in his gaze that she'd seen then. None of the deep light that had disturbed her the night of the dance fest.

And thank goodness for that, she told herself, ignoring a small stirring of chagrin. Hadn't they agreed that in the circumstances it was better to remain just friends? Anything else would be less than sensible. Quinn had said when he'd asked her to accompany him as his wife that she should regard it as a job. Living in artificial intimacy and in the heady, perfume-laden air of the tropics, it wasn't surprising that a faint sexual tension underlaid their relationship. But a temporary madness might lead to an even bigger mess than the one she'd run away from. And a temporary madness, surely, was all that her feelings for Quinn amounted to.

'What's the matter?' he asked her as they stopped before one of the tables.

'Nothing. The pineapple juice looks nice.'

Quinn poured it for her, and another for himself. 'Cheers,' he said, raising his glass. 'I hope you're enjoying the party.'

'It's interesting.' Stefanie looked around at the colourful crowd, most of them in bright island prints. She was wearing a cool, short-sleeved white dress that complemented the faint tan she'd acquired despite a liberal use of sun block. 'Funny, isn't it? A few months ago I would never have imagined that now I'd be in a place like this, with...'

'A man like me?' he finished, the skin about his eyes crinkling. 'Is it so bad?'

'It's not bad at all, as you know very well. I love Busiata. What about you?'

'I have no regrets.' He lowered his eyelids and sipped at his drink.

'None?'

He looked beyond her, his eyes glazing in thought. 'You were right. It's probably a good thing that Noelle found out before we committed ourselves to marriage that she was making a mistake.'

'I hope she hasn't made another one,' Stefanie said involuntarily, her brow creasing.

Quinn glanced at her curiously as they moved away from the table. 'You worry about her?'

'We've been best friends for a long time. I can't help being fond of her in spite of...everything.'

'You've known Bryan a long time too.'

'Yes.'

His mouth tightened. 'Are you still *fond* of him?' His voice sounded harsh, almost sneering, although he hadn't raised it.

Stefanie hesitated. It dawned on her that if she ever had been truly in love with Bryan, she wasn't any longer. The sudden insight took her breath, gave her a feeling of freedom, a lift of the heart.

Raising her eyes to Quinn, she centred on him a

clear, almost smiling look. 'I'm still fond of him,' she acknowledged, carefully examining her emotions, feeling honesty was important. 'I've known him almost as long as I have Noelle, and I can't just wipe out all those years. All my feelings for him.'

She paused again, sorting the words to articulate exactly how she felt. If she stated baldly that she'd fallen out of love with Bryan, it would sound as though she was giving Quinn a sexual invitation, wouldn't it? And she wasn't sure how he would receive that, even if she dared do it.

Quinn's eyes had gone dark. 'So...' he drawled. But she never found out what he intended to say, because they were hailed by an acquaintance and Quinn paused to talk. But as they stood there his arm came about her waist in a rather proprietorial way, and when they moved on again he didn't remove it.

Later there was entertainment—a brass band, traditional dancing and a performance of precision marching by the palace guard, while the king and queen watched from chairs set on the palace portico. Afterwards the king made a speech, and then people began to drift off home.

The afternoon was waning. As their scooters puttered side by side along the road near the seashore, the sun was lowering, throwing a pink sheen on the water and colouring the sky. Stefanie slowed to look, and Quinn said, 'Want to stop?'

'Yes.'

They swerved off the road onto a bumpy flattish area, and brought their machines to a halt facing the sea.

'Let's walk.' Stefanie bent down to pull off her sandals.

'If you like.' Quinn swung off his scooter, then removed his own shoes and rolled his trousers to the ankle. They went down the short, shallow slope to the white, gritty coral sand, and strolled along near the water.

Soon the road was hidden by palm trees and undergrowth crowding the edge of the sand. The few ribbons of cloud in the sky turned fiery, and a wave foamed in a semi-circle ahead of them, leaving an arc of pink bubbles behind. Stefanie paused and popped one with her bare toe.

Quinn stopped too, and looped an arm about her shoulders as they watched the sun touch the sea, then inch below the horizon. Another wave washed over their ankles but they scarcely noticed.

When the last sliver of burning gold disappeared Quinn said quietly, 'Enough for you?'

'I suppose so,' Stefanie said regretfully. 'That was a wonderful sunset.' It had soothed her soul, and she liked the feel of Quinn's sheltering arm.

'Sure was.' He turned without taking his arm from her, and they began walking back the way they'd come. Already it was dusk.

A couple of fishermen were wading into the water, a net carried between them. The palm trees rustled and clacked in a breeze drifting from the sea, the lagoon flattening now and turning leaden, colourless. Stefanie gave a small shiver.

'Are you cold?' Quinn's palm rubbed at the slight gooseflesh on her arm.

'It's just got suddenly cooler now the sun's gone. But I haven't been really cold since we got here. No one could be cold on Busiata.'

'No,' he said. 'No one could.'

Something sharp pierced her foot, and she drew in a breath and stopped walking.

'What is it?' Quinn's arm slipped from her shoulder to grip her arm as she bent, lifting her foot.

'I don't know. I stepped on something.'

'Let me see.' He went down on one knee, taking her ankle in his hands as she steadied herself on his shoulder. 'It's bleeding.'

'Not much.'

'Damn, I can't see properly in this light. Don't put your foot down. I'll carry you.'

'It's nothing—you've no need—'

But he was already standing, swinging her into his arms. 'You don't want any of this sand getting into the wound. Coral poisoning can be really nasty.'

She put her arms around his neck and he walked over the sand to the scooters, staggering slightly when his feet sank into the soft, dry part of the beach.

He grunted, and Stefanie laughed softly. 'You won't drop me, will you?'

'I won't let you go—promise.' He smiled down at her. She quelled a desire to tighten her arms and bring his face closer, his lips to hers.

Being held like this was arousing sensations that she knew were entirely inappropriate.

He reached the firmer ground and lowered her to the seat of her scooter, then bent again to examine her foot. He fumbled in his pockets and produced a folded handkerchief, shook it out, and tied it about her foot in a makeshift bandage. 'Will you be able to drive home, or do you want to ride with me?'

She remembered the last time she'd been pillion passenger, and crushed the thought and the piercing, unexpected longing it brought with it. 'I'll be all right.'

When they got back to the house she insisted on limping inside herself, but let Quinn clean the wound and bathe it in disinfectant while she perched on the wide edge of the big porcelain bath.

Then he sat beside her and held her foot in his lap while he patted it dry with a clean towel and pressed a large plaster over it. 'I think it's a coral cut. We'll have to keep an eye on it and hope it doesn't become infected, though there doesn't seem to be anything in it.'

'Not now,' Stefanie said wryly. 'You were very thorough.'

'Did it hurt?' Quinn looked up. 'You never murmured.'

'It had to be done. No use making a fuss.'

'I'm sorry if it was painful. You're very brave.'

He still held her foot, and unexpectedly he bent his head and dropped a kiss on the upper curve of the arch.

Stefanie almost choked on a breath, and he lifted his head, casting her a single, glittering glance. 'There,' he said lightly. 'All better.'

CHAPTER EIGHT

SHAKEN, Stefanie got to her feet, or rather her one
good foot, gingerly lowering the other to the ground.
His arm came about her again, and she said, 'I can
manage.'

'Sure? I'll clean up in here.' His tone was quite
casual, but she'd seen what was in his eyes before he
hid it from her. She hobbled into her room, went over
to the bed, and was sitting on the edge of it when he
came in a few minutes later.

'Can I get you anything?' he asked. 'Or help you
to the dining room?' His face was mask-like now, his
eyes hooded.

'I'm not hungry.' They'd given Winnie an extra
day off so that she too could celebrate the sovereign's
birthday. 'There was such a lot of food there today.'

'I don't really want any more to eat either.' He
strolled to the window, looking out at the gathering
darkness, and then turned and leaned on the frame,
his hands in his pockets as he studied her. 'Sure
you're okay?'

'Yes, thank you. You'd make a good nurse.'

And a good husband. Noelle must have been crazy
to leave him. He was all any woman could want—
kind, considerate, strong, capable. 'Is there anything
you can't do?'

He laughed softly. 'Plenty. For one thing, apparently I can't hold a woman.' He didn't sound sorry
for himself, just wryly self-deprecating.

125

'I'm sure that's not true.' Stefanie could hardly see his face now, with his back to the remaining light. She too must be in shadow. She said, 'Noelle had never been the faithful type.'

'I suppose not. When we met she was with someone else.'

'But she didn't want to be.'

'Did Noelle tell you that?'

'She said you stepped in when her boyfriend was drunk and threatening her. She was awfully impressed at how you handled the situation. And grateful. Maybe she mistook that for love.'

'You could be right,' he agreed. After a moment he said, 'What about you, Stefanie? Are you the faithful type?'

'I think so.' She had been sure she'd have had no trouble keeping her wedding vows—the ones she would have exchanged with Bryan. 'I believe in commitment to one person. In keeping promises.'

'Even if the other person doesn't share that commitment, and breaks promises? Could you still love them?'

'Love isn't something that can be turned on and off like a tap.'

'Possibly it's something that dries up and withers for lack of nourishment and support, though,' Quinn suggested, propping one foot against the other ankle.

'I suppose that can happen.'

'But not to you?'

'I hope not.'

He was silent for a moment. 'You said you didn't intend to let Bryan ruin your life.'

'I don't. I'll get over what happened and move on, in time.' She hesitated, but this conversation was already touching on the intimate. 'Was Noelle the first woman to let you down?'

'I'd never been engaged before. Never asked anyone to marry me.'

So why Noelle? She was so different from him. Thinking aloud, Stefanie said, 'She's very pretty. And...sweet.' Noelle never lost her temper, always saw the good in other people. Sometimes Stefanie had thought she was too trusting, too ready to believe in people, too generous with her emotions, and that was why her love affairs never lasted.

'She was,' Quinn agreed unemotionally, 'irresistible.'

Stefanie swallowed, finding that her throat hurt. 'I can imagine.'

'Can you?' He straightened. 'I think I'll have a swim. But I'm afraid you'd better keep that foot out of the water for a day or two. Will you be all right?'

'Yes. I'm not really crippled. Enjoy your swim.'

She stayed where she was for several minutes after he'd left the room, until she heard him close the back door leading to the pool area.

After a while she got up and tested her foot. It was less sore now, but it didn't appreciate her putting weight on it. She limped into the kitchen and poured herself a glass of water to ease the dryness in her throat. Outside she could hear Quinn vigorously swimming laps. She pictured his lithe body powering through the water, the way the muscles in his shoulders flexed, and how he looked when he came out of the pool, with his hair slicked to seal-like blackness, his long legs streaming with water, and his lean flanks and the unmistakable maleness encased in wet nylon.

Her hand tightened on the glass, and warmth spread

through her. What was she doing, fantasising about Quinn?

Quinn…her husband. Legally.

And that was all, she reminded herself. He'd made it perfectly clear that he had no need of anything more than her signature on a piece of paper and her presence at his side for six months or so. No strings, no permanence.

And yet he'd said he was finding his vow of celibacy difficult, and sometimes the way he looked at her…

The way he'd looked at Noelle? No, it wasn't the same.

And that ought to make her tread warily. Otherwise she could get herself into a real mess.

She was so deep in thought she hadn't realised that the sounds of splashing outside had stopped. How long had she been standing there with the empty glass in her hand, staring at nothing?

Quinn opened the door and stepped into the room, his hair roughly rubbed half-dry and the towel slung around his hips.

'Did you get hungry after all?' he enquired, closing the door behind him.

'Just thirsty.' She put the glass down on the counter. 'How was the pool?'

'It helped cool me off. How's the foot?'

'Better, but I can't walk on it yet.'

'Take it easy.' His gaze lingered on her bare feet, then swept back to her face. 'We won't go out tomorrow.'

In deference to local custom they didn't use the scooters on Sundays, instead usually taking a long, leisurely stroll. She nodded.

'I'd better change,' Quinn said abruptly. 'I'm dripping.'

She couldn't help watching him cross the room, covertly admiring the masculine grace of his barefoot walk.

Unexpectedly he swung round as he reached the doorway, catching her eye. His eyelids flickered and she saw his shoulders brace. 'Don't look at me like that,' he said.

Stefanie's cheeks flooded with heat.

'Unless,' he added softly, 'you want me to do something about it.'

It was only fifteen minutes or so since he'd told her he'd found Noelle irresistible. Yet despite the occasional flare of sexual awareness—no doubt ignited more by proximity and frustration than anything— he'd had very little trouble resisting Stefanie.

Her chin lifting, she said, 'I don't need any favours from you, Quinn.'

'Well,' he said with a crooked grin, 'any time you change your mind...'

Stefanie shook her head. 'I don't think so.'

He shrugged slightly and turned again, disappearing into the passageway.

Her heart thumping, Stefanie gripped the edge of the sink. Damn, he knew how she reacted to him. As any normal woman would, with him swanning around half-naked like that. How could she have let him see it?

Friends, she'd said. And Quinn had said, Maybe.

And yet he was the one who had dictated the terms of their bargain.

He'd known she wouldn't have agreed otherwise,

she guessed. Had he, even then, thought this might happen? Maybe counted on it?

No, of course not. He'd made it very clear at the start that he had no such expectation, and when he'd kissed her he had apologised sincerely. Quinn hadn't planned for this any more than she had. It was something they should probably have allowed for but that had taken them both unawares.

She went back to her room, unwilling to face him again tonight, and was already in bed and reading when she heard him later in the bathroom. When the water ceased to run there was a short silence, and then he knocked on her door.

'Yes?'

He opened the door but didn't move into the room. 'Anything I can do for you before I go to bed?'

'Thanks, no. I have everything I need.'

'I wish I could say the same.' He paused, watching her. 'Goodnight, then.'

'Goodnight, Quinn.' She remained staring at the door until the light beneath it went black, then tried to return her attention to her romantic novel. But she kept losing track of the plot, and seeing Quinn's face instead of the hero's.

When she came out the next morning he had breakfast ready on the terrace, and was lounging in a chair, staring at the pool. He looked up. 'Ah, there you are. Ready for breakfast?'

'Have you been waiting for me?'

'The food can't get cold, and I like having company at breakfast.' He got up and pulled out a chair for her.

She wondered if he was accustomed to feminine

company at breakfast, but stopped herself from asking.

Quinn resumed his seat. 'I thought we'd have a lazy day.'

Stefanie dug a fork into a piece of banana among the mixed fruit on her plate. 'Maybe we'll have visitors.'

'That's possible.' The locals were very friendly and hospitable, but unless specifically pressed they seldom came to the house.

When breakfast was over Quinn insisted on doing the dishes alone, after settling Stefanie on a shaded lounger with a book that he fetched from her room.

A little later he returned, pulled up a low table and put a covered jug of iced juice and a glass beside her. 'I should have a look at that foot,' he told her.

'It only hurts when I walk on it.'

'Still, I'll get the first-aid box and renew the dressing.'

He did the job with the same competence he'd exhibited the day before, but this time didn't follow it up with a kiss.

Then he brought his laptop and sat at the outdoor table, apparently absorbed in his work. Stefanie watched him for a while, then wrenched her attention back to her book.

When she heard him quietly swear she looked up. 'What's wrong?'

'The battery's run out. Can I get you anything while I'm fetching another one?'

'I should write another letter to my family. If you could bring me a pad from my bedside table, and a pen...?'

He brought them for her, and inserted the new battery into his computer. Stefanie put down her book and began writing her letter. At least she had plenty to write about, describing the island, the king's family, the people and her work.

After her first mail reached them, she'd received an agitated missive from her mother, with an excited note from Tracey and a scrawled note from her father, and Gwenda had sent a separate, restrained but puzzled letter. Stefanie hoped her cheerful weekly letters and the two phone calls she'd made had allayed their fears for her.

Looking up as she turned to a second page of description of the king's birthday celebrations, she found Quinn's gaze on her.

Quinn returned his attention to the screen before him, and she went on writing.

It should have been a restful scene, two people absorbed in their separate tasks in companionable silence, with the sun shining on the clear water of the pool and the bees humming among the hibiscus.

Instead Stefanie found herself intensely aware of the way the pool ripples reflected a glancing pattern of light on Quinn's casual cream shirt, of the slight movement as he flexed his leg under the table, and the tiny sounds of his fingers hitting the computer keys. Then he sat back and thrust a hand through his hair, giving a short sigh.

His eyes were dark and brooding. Suddenly he pushed back his chair, the metal feet screeching on the tiles, and stood up. 'I need a drink,' he muttered. 'A real one. How about you?'

Stefanie shook her head. 'I'll stick with juice, thanks.'

He strode off to the house, and when he came out

again with a glass half filled with amber liquid she had the feeling he'd already downed one.

Looking grim, he placed the glass beside his computer and went on working until after twelve.

Finally he picked up the almost empty glass, swilled the melted ice in the bottom, and tossed the remains down his throat. 'Lunch?'

Stefanie had finished her letter and returned to her book. She swung her legs off the lounger. 'I'll make lunch.'

'You're sure?' He watched critically as she began to limp towards the kitchen.

'I'm okay, honestly. Don't worry about me. Are sandwiches all right?'

'Fine. Be careful.'

She heaped a platter with salad sandwiches, and added two side plates and a bowl of fruit to a tray. When she appeared in the doorway to the patio, Quinn pushed his computer aside and leapt up. 'You should have called me to carry that!'

'I managed perfectly well.' Stefanie put a couple of sandwich triangles on her empty plate and retired back to the lounger.

Quinn passed her some more later, and when there were only two sandwiches left on the serving dish asked, 'Want one?'

'Thanks.'

She made to move, but Quinn said, 'Stay there,' and brought the serving plate to her.

Instead of returning to the table he put the platter down beside her and sat on the lounger near her legs while he finished the last sandwich. 'I'll take your plate,' he offered, his hand going out, but she was already sitting forward, prepared to place the empty

plate with the serving dish, and his fingers acciden-
tally brushed across her breast.

Stefanie made a tiny, choked sound and dropped
the plate on the tiles, where it smashed loudly into
three pieces.

Quinn said something under his breath. 'My fault.'

'I dropped it.'

'Yes,' he said, and dragged his gaze from the broken pieces of china to her face. 'You're no prude,
Stefanie.'

'I was startled. I know it was an accident,' she assured him. 'You didn't mean to...'

'No...I didn't.' His gaze slid momentarily to the
breast that still tingled from his inadvertent touch.
'Only startled?' he murmured.

Stefanie refused to look down. She knew quite well
what he meant. Her cotton blouse was thin and he'd
have had to be blind not to notice her reaction. Her
bra felt tight, her skin supersensitive.

Trying to stay calm, she said huskily, 'It's just a
physical reflex.'

'You're not the only one.'

She did look down then, at him. And away again
as soon as she realised what she was doing.

Quinn gave a small laugh. He took her hand in his,
not so firmly that she couldn't have pulled away if
she'd wanted to. Only she didn't.

Her breath was stuck in her throat, but his eyes
steadily held hers. He placed her hand at the top of
his thigh, and still she didn't resist. Then he moved
it to the apex, and through the sun-warmed fabric of
his trousers she felt his arousal surge against her palm
as his hand cradled hers.

Her heart thundering, she bit down hard on her

lower lip, and Quinn closed his eyes, threw his head back, and let out a long, shuddering sigh.

'Quinn.' Her voice sounded reedy and wavering.

He turned his head, his eyes opening slowly, glittering at her. 'Stefanie.'

'No.' She got the word past her trembling lips somehow.

She moved her hand inside his, trying to lift it away, and after a moment he helped her, but his fingers curled strongly about hers, holding her in an almost painful grip. 'No?' he repeated harshly. 'You're as aroused as I am.' His eyes raked her face, and then lingered openly on the tell-tale outline under her shirt.

'You're a very sexy man,' she admitted in a low voice, 'and we're living in…in an unnatural situation here. But you don't really want me.'

His brows rose. 'I thought I'd just given you—if you'll excuse the expression—some hard evidence to the contrary.'

Another time she might have laughed, even though the humour in his eyes held a definite note of satire. But this was too serious for laughter. 'You've been deprived for months. It was an impulse that you'll probably regret later.'

'Only if you did.' He released her and stood up, thrusting his hands into his pockets. 'But I certainly won't force you. I think I'd better have a cold shower.' He stooped and gathered up the plates and the shards of china, before making for the house.

Just before reaching the door he turned. 'By the way,' he said in a deceptively mild tone, 'you're wrong, you know. This was no sudden impulse. Yesterday you said I was like a dog in the manger, implying that I don't want you for myself, but you couldn't be more wrong about that. I do want you, Stefanie—very much. I have done for weeks now. And I think you know it.'

Stefanie stared after him, while the heat left her cheeks and her heartbeat gradually steadied.

Be sensible. Yes, he 'wants' you—but only in a superficial, physical way, and perhaps for a bit of comfort.

The same way you want him?

Well…but men are different.

Oh, yes, the inner voice jeered at her. What's so different about it? He was right, you were just as aroused as he was. You nearly fainted with pleasure when he put your hand on him, went weak at the knees, knowing you could do that to him.

And if you didn't feel something for the man, you know very well you'd have hated it.

Stefanie dropped her head into her hands. Was it possible she was falling in love with Quinn?

He was away a long time, and when he came back he cast her a swift, unreadable glance and went to lean on one of the supporting posts of the pergola, his face more than half averted from her, his arms folded.

After a while he said, 'Should I apologise?'

'There's no need. I'm sorry if I led you on—or let you lead me.'

He turned his head, smiling at her a little. 'If I don't have to apologise, you certainly don't. I did promise you I wouldn't expect you to be a real wife. You're entitled to insist on sticking to the terms of the contract.'

It was a bit like stepping under a cold shower herself. If she'd needed any reinforcement of the fact that his wanting her had nothing to do with loving her, he'd just brutally given it. They had a contract, and it would run out in three more months. Then Quinn expected to be free. And after the requisite two years to obtain a formal divorce they would have no further ties to each other.

A gaping black hole seemed to open up inside her at the thought. She stood up. 'I'm going inside. It's getting too hot here.'

Quinn gave her a searching look, then his eyes went to the ground in front of her and he said, 'Don't move!'

Startled, she stood still as he strode over, bent, and straightened again with a small, sharp triangle of china in his fingers. 'I missed that bit. You don't want another sore foot.'

'No. Thank you.' Automatically she looked down in case there were more pieces. Quinn was doing the same. Then he stepped back. 'All clear, I think.'

She went away from him, into the dimness of the interior, at first hardly able to see a thing. Stopping to orient herself, she glanced back and saw Quinn standing where she had left him, his right hand tightly clenched, his shoulders rigid.

Stefanie wrenched her eyes away and blundered along the passage.

She spent the remainder of the afternoon in the cool garden room at the front of the house, trying to continue her reading but mostly staring into space.

The following day while Quinn was efficiently dressing her foot after work she noticed that he too had a plaster on, across the centre of his palm.

'What did you do to your hand?' she asked him.

'It's nothing. There, that's healing nicely. No sign of infection.' He turned to get a fresh plaster and press it over her wound.

'Thanks. Can I do the same for you?'

'It's a clean cut and I can easily look after it myself.'

'We're a right pair,' she commented as he put away the first-aid box. 'Are you sure—'

'I told you, it's all right!'

Stefanie blinked, and Quinn closed the cupboard with a bang, then turned. 'I didn't mean to snap at you. Thanks for asking, but forget it, will you?' He sounded suddenly weary.

She didn't mention his hand again, but later that night she recalled that yesterday he'd picked up the nasty little fragment of broken china and held it in his palm, and how when she'd looked back at him a minute later he'd been standing with his hand closed tightly into a fist.

Within a couple of days Quinn wasn't wearing a plaster any more. Her foot took longer to heal completely, but she had no ill effects.

Quinn often shut himself up in his bedroom at night, working on the laptop, and Stefanie took to bringing work home too, boxes full of papers and books that she spread on the dining table and sat sorting through, making notes.

The next time the prince dropped in to check on the progress of the archiving project, she told him, 'I need a translator for the Busiatan documents. And I'd like to suggest that someone should write a history of the island. All the material is here now.'

'Perhaps you would be interested?'

Stefanie shook her head. 'It should be done by a local. A person who knows both languages and was brought up in the culture. I'd probably miss things, or put wrong interpretations on them.'

'I'll find someone,' he promised. 'Our civil service is full of educated people with not enough to do.'

A few days later the prince came into the library with Tom Tualala at his side, the young man looking pleased and eager. 'Here is our translator and historian, Mrs Branson.'

Despite his talkative nature, Tom proved a godsend. He was energetic and willing, and Stefanie handed over all the documents written in the native language for him to classify and make notes from. He was a keen researcher, and if he was puzzled by some archaic term or obscure reference, he would take it to an older islander and make sure he had it right.

She was enthusiastically describing Tom's thoroughness and translation skills to Quinn over dinner one night when he looked up as he swallowed the last of his roast pork, then said dryly, 'And he's also smitten with you.'

'Oh, don't be silly, he just likes his job. The prince said half the civil servants don't have enough to do. This is probably the first time Tom's been really challenged since he got his degree. He's loving it.'

'So long as that's all he loves.'

Stefanie shook her head. 'You're barking up the wrong tree.' She finished her meal, pushed her plate aside and reached for a glass of water.

'First you call me a dog in the manger, and now I'm barking up the wrong tree,' Quinn remarked. 'Do you have any more canine analogies you'd like to apply to me?'

Stefanie gave him a look of trepidation and saw the ironic humour in his eyes. She was so relieved that she couldn't help laughing.

Quinn sat back in his chair. 'That's better,' he said.

She knew he'd done it deliberately to ease the tension that had made living together so uncomfortable lately. A tight band that seemed to have been fastened immovably about her chest ever since that fraught Sunday afternoon relaxed a trifle. 'Yes,' she said simply, letting him know that she understood perfectly. On impulse she added, 'I do like you, Quinn.'

His smile turned a little sardonic. 'Like.'

'If I hadn't I would never have come here with you. You make me feel quite…safe.'

A strange expression killed the smile on his lips. 'It seems to be my forte.'

Stefanie clearly remembered his fiercely protective attitude towards his ex-fiancée. 'Well, it's nice,' she said lamely.

'Nice.' Scorn coloured his voice. 'Hell.'

'Pardon?'

'Never mind.' He looked up as Winnie entered the room with a bowl of compote for dessert. When she'd gone again he turned the conversation to something else.

Every weekday Quinn collected any mail from the post office in the capital. Stefanie didn't receive much, but her mother sent a regular letter along with any mail that had arrived at home for her. Mostly it was from her bank or the tax department—or occasionally some firm from whom she'd once bought something, assuring her that she was one of their most valued customers. She had told very few people where she was, and given the address only to her family.

She was sitting in the garden room late one afternoon, combing tangles out of her damp hair, when Quinn came home and straight to her.

'Been swimming already?' he asked her.

'Mm. It was so hot.'

'Mail for you.' He handed her an envelope. 'I think I'll have a dip myself.'

When he came back, freshly changed into a T-shirt and cotton pants, the envelope had fallen to the floor and her fingers held the letter on her lap, but her gaze was fixed on the tall thrusting palm trees silhouetted against the sky, with the gleam and glitter of the sea peeking intermittently between their spiky leaves.

'Are you all right?' he asked her, stopping near her chair.

'Yes.' Not taking her eyes from the view outside, she said, 'They're married. Bryan and Noelle—my mother says they got married.'

CHAPTER NINE

QUINN didn't move for several seconds. 'Well…' he said flatly, at last. 'That's that, then.'

He went to stand with his back to the windows, where he could see her. 'How do you feel about it?'

Stefanie dragged her gaze from the distant horizon to his face—a face that was quite expressionless, giving her no clue to his emotions. 'As if a door has closed.'

'Leaving you out in the cold?' He paused, and she wondered if he had just described his own reaction. 'They say when one door closes another opens.'

'I know.' She didn't feel cold, just empty and oddly expectant—as if she'd finally shed invisible fetters, but was waiting for something. She didn't know what that was. 'I'm all right,' she said, reassuring him. 'How about you?'

A shoulder briefly lifted. 'I don't give a damn what they do,' he told her. 'I wish Noelle every happiness.'

She wondered if it was true. Looking away from him, she carefully folded the letter, but couldn't find the envelope. Quinn moved swiftly, picking it up from the floor where she'd dropped it, and handed it to her.

'Would you like to go for a walk?' he asked.

'Yes.' She hadn't known what she needed until he suggested it, but something physical to do was exactly right. 'Yes, let's.'

'I'll tell Winnie to leave dinner for us and go off duty, in case we're late getting back.'

He held her hand as they walked, going uphill first by tacit consent, following the road that wound among the trees, keeping in the shade although the power of the sun was waning now. Once Quinn said, 'Am I going too fast?'

'No.' Even though she could feel a film of sweat at her temples and her breath was coming fast, she didn't want to slow down. This wasn't the time for a leisurely stroll.

They passed a little group of houses, and people waved at them from the verandahs, children calling greetings. They waved back but didn't stop. Eventually they came to a place where the road dropped sheerly away, and the trees were low enough that they could sit on a small grassy area and watch the sun dip to the limitless ocean.

Quinn's arm came around her shoulders, and she moved closer and hooked her own arm about his waist. Something had just ended for him too. And despite his apparently unemotional reception of the news, maybe he needed comfort.

When the last lingering colour began to leach from the sea Quinn stirred. 'We'd better get back.'

'Yes,' she agreed, though reluctantly.

He pulled her to her feet, then unexpectedly dipped his head and pressed his mouth to hers.

It was a strangely desperate-seeming kiss, with an underlying fierceness about it, but lasted only a moment before he wordlessly released her and took her hand in his.

The downhill walk was quicker, and the temperature cooler. The lights of the house looked welcoming as they entered, and in the kitchen Winnie had left the meal ready to serve.

'Why don't we eat here?' Stefanie suggested.

'Good idea. I'll shower first, though.'

She took another short swim while he was in the shower, then tied a cool cotton sarong about her body, tucking in the ends above her breasts. The tiles were cool to her bare feet as she padded about putting the meal on the table.

Quinn came back in a fresh Polo shirt and light sand-coloured pants, but no shoes.

They didn't talk much, clearing up afterwards together. The strange, waiting sense of expectancy hadn't left her—if anything it had grown more intense. She watched Quinn hang up a tea-towel, aligning it precisely on its rail, and then he turned to her and said, 'What do you want to do now?'

I want to make love with you.

The thought was so compelling, so clear, she felt as if she'd spoken it aloud, the echo of it vibrating in the air.

Courage failing, she said instead, 'I don't know. It's too early to go to bed.'

'I guess. But I don't want to work tonight.'

'Neither do I.'

He seemed to hesitate. 'Can we talk?'

'Of course.' He'd given her what she needed earlier. Maybe what he'd needed then too. But if now he wanted to talk she was certainly ready to accommodate him. 'Shall we go back to the garden room?'

They sat in semi-darkness, the light in the room behind them on, but none where they settled themselves on either side of the small glass table, both facing the deeper darkness outside.

An extravagant display of winking and glittering stars, distant and flashy, spread across the sky above the graceful silhouettes of the palm trees. One bright point of light left its place and streaked in a long arc across the blackness.

'Oh, look!' Stefanie involuntarily pointed. And even as she did so the shooting star died to nothingness.

'It's supposed to be a sign, isn't it?' Quinn said.

'I guess.' A sign of a love that died? Something bright and shining that inevitably burned itself out?

Maybe falling in love was always like that. A temporary, blinding flash and sparkle that left nothing behind but a lump of cold rock floating aimlessly in endless darkness.

No. Her parents' love was perhaps not as incandescent as it might once have been, but its banked fire had warmed her childhood and still kept their marriage strong.

Sometimes you had to trust life. Trust another person. Even after a betrayal by someone you'd loved. You couldn't live on bitterness and suspicion, afraid of letting yourself be hurt again, afraid of living.

They had been sitting quietly side by side for some time when Quinn stirred. 'Stefanie...maybe it isn't the right time, but then there may never be a right time to ask you this.'

'Ask me what?' She looked at him, and he turned his head slowly to face her. 'Forgive me if you find it crass and...unwelcome at this moment. But to me it seems right.' He paused, and she saw his shoulders move, heard him breathe in. His voice deepened. 'I want to make our marriage real. I want you to be my wife...my lover.'

There was a long, throbbing silence. A winged insect threw itself against the window, blatting at it several times, then flew off into the night. Stefanie moistened her lips. 'It isn't unwelcome,' she said. She dropped her gaze and discovered her hands were tightly clamped together in her lap. Carefully she looked up. 'It isn't unwelcome at all.'

He moved so abruptly she thought he was going to leap up and snatch her into his arms. Instead he held out his hand to her, and she unclamped her fingers and put hers into his strong clasp.

'Thank you,' he said. 'I'm not asking you to say you love me, but I hope that may come, in time.'

Stefanie swallowed. He wasn't saying he loved her either, she noted, shaking off a faint chill that threatened to spoil the moment. When she'd passed on her mother's news he'd said he didn't give a damn, but Noelle—beautiful, enchanting, irresistible Noelle—must still have a small place in his mind, his heart. Perhaps a large part of it.

No doubt he was speaking for himself too when he said he hoped love would come in time. He wouldn't lie to her, and for that she could only be grateful.

'Yes,' she said, saying yes to the unknown, to her feelings, to trusting him, to looking forward and not back. To letting go of the past and loving Quinn. 'Yes.'

He stood up then, and pulled her to her feet. 'There's no hurry,' he said, 'but I'd like to seal this in the time-honoured way.'

He drew her into his arms quite slowly, and she let her body arch against the enclosing curve of his right arm, her face lifting to his.

The light fell on him, and she looked up and saw

his expression was grave and questioning. Then he bent his head and she closed her eyes and Quinn's lips found hers in a kiss full of tenderness and promise.

The chill of apprehension melted away in a warm tide of desire as she returned the kiss in kind, her lips parting willingly under the pressure of his mouth, her head tucked into his shoulder when he gathered her closer.

His mouth was firm but determinedly gentle, and after a minute or so he kissed her forehead and murmured against her skin, 'Okay?'

'Yes.' She could dimly see the pulse at the base of his throat, a tiny trip-hammer beating on a level with her mouth. Impulsively she put her lips to the spot.

She felt the shudder that passed through Quinn's body, and the quick, audible breath that he took. 'Don't,' he ground out. 'Unless…'

Stefanie drew back, raising her head but curving her arms about his neck. 'Unless?' she queried softly, and without giving him a chance to reply she reached up and pressed her mouth again to his.

He gave a sound that was half a groan, half a muffled laugh, and then he was kissing her with unalloyed passion, opening her mouth fully, exploring it, holding her tight while her body sang with taut, heart-stopping anticipation, tiny ripples of excitement running everywhere over her skin.

Her hand spread across the back of his neck, her fingers enjoying the unexpected silkiness of his hair, then slipping into the collar of his shirt.

Quinn gave another little grunt, and the hand at her waist moved lower and behind her, lifting her to him as he shifted his feet, until she could feel unmistakably the physical effect the kiss was having on him.

Boldly she moved against him, letting him know she wanted him too.

He wrenched his mouth away from hers once more, and in a thickened, uneven voice demanded, 'Stefanie—are you sure? Do you want this right now?'

She still had her arms about him. Hiding her hot face against his shirt, she said, 'I'm sure.' She had never wanted anything so much—so very much.

He tugged at her hair, gathering a handful of it so that she had to lift her face and look at him. His eyes blazed, studying her. Then he nodded, as if what he saw satisfied any doubts. 'Then let's go find a bed,' he said.

He took her to his, his arm holding her close to him while they walked. Stefanie wondered if she were dreaming, and yet every sense was alert. She could hear the small clacking sound of a breeze-blown palm tree outside the window, the clear call of some night bird—even, she was sure, the distant waves hurling themselves onto the reef. The scent of frangipani and jasmine drifted in through the insect screens, and she could smell the soap that Quinn had used in the shower, mingled with his own unique, male aroma that had entered her nostrils while she was kissing him, a potent aphrodisiac.

The wooden slat blinds were pulled up and starlight filled the room, almost bright enough to read by. Quinn didn't switch even the bedside lamp on, but led her over to the window where the light spilled in on them, and said, 'I want to undress you.'

'And I you,' she answered him. Already her hands were lifting his Polo shirt away from his trousers, sliding it up over his ribs. But he didn't let her complete the action, instead hauling the shirt over his head himself and dropping it on the floor.

She ran her fingertips lightly over his chest while his hands rested on her waist, his thumbs caressing her ribcage.

Her leisurely exploration reached the buckle of his belt and she began working it free, and his hands went to tug at the knot of her sarong.

He loosened it and the fabric fell to her hips.

She continued with her self-imposed task, trying to ignore the way he was looking at her, but feeling her breasts peak and tingle although he wasn't touching her any more.

The leather tongue of his belt slipped from the metal buckle, and she fumbled for the zip of his pants, heard the putter of fabric on the mat before he kicked the trousers away. Then he pulled the sarong down over her hips, letting it float to the floor.

He smoothed away the triangle of cotton she wore, his hands lingering on the flare of her hips, the smooth skin of her thighs, until the minimal garment joined the little heap of clothing at their feet.

And then she turned her attention to the briefs that rode low on his lean hips, and knelt to pull them down over his ankles.

'Stefanie!' He touched her hair, and then he was kneeling too, his hands moving from her hair to cup her face for a fiercely possessive kiss, before shaping the curve of her shoulder and neck, and at last, resting on her yearning breasts.

Her head went back, her eyes closed, lips parted, the sensations he aroused almost unbearable as his hands cradled her flesh, his thumbs finding the proud buds at the centre, and then his mouth was on hers again, seeking and hungry, and she wound her arms about his neck to keep her balance, and to keep him with her. Close to her. Closer.

They were still not close enough, and when he scooped her onto his bare thighs, his hands finding the shallow groove of her spine, the roundness of her behind, the blood drummed in her veins and she cried out against his mouth.

He tore it momentarily away from hers. 'Are you all right?'

'*Yes,*' she said frantically. 'Oh, yes!'

He kissed her again, more deeply, and next time he stopped his head dipped and she felt his mouth on her breasts, the faint rasp of his shaven cheek, the delicious tug of his lips and tongue. This time her cry of pleasure spiralled into the darkness and she held him to her, her fingers buried in his hair.

Then his mouth was back on hers, and his strong arms lifted her, bringing her upright with him, his erection pressing against her. 'The bed,' he muttered, and swung her into his arms, and she felt the rush of slightly cooler air before he lowered her to the softness of the mattress.

He flung off the covers and settled her on the cool cotton sheet.

'Should I slow down?' he asked as he lay beside her.

'Why?' Stefanie demanded starkly, turning to run her hand over him, tracing the outline of his ribs, his hip, the taut muscles of his thigh. 'Do you want to slow down?'

'I want to do this right…for you.' He returned the

caress, his fingers awakening sensitive, quivering nerves all over her.

'It *is* right for me,' she assured him. 'It's lovely.'

'*You* are lovely,' he replied, his voice deep and not quite even. 'You have a beautiful body, Stefanie.'

She wouldn't think about Noelle and her lush, fragile femininity—she wouldn't. Winding her arms about his neck, she kissed him, willing him to forget everything, everyone but her, arching against him until he made a guttural sound in his throat and pulled away from her.

For a few brief moments he wasn't touching her any more, and she waited, hardly breathing, until his shadow lifted over her and she said, 'Yes, now!' And cried out with relief as she felt the smooth glide of his passage to her inner softness.

And she welcomed him, welcomed the hard thrust of him, the waves of pleasure that rippled through her body, gathered into a flood, a burst of light, until her head was flung back against the pillow as she writhed against him, felt him surge and peak and ride over the crest with her in his arms.

When the sweet storm abated they were both panting.

Still holding her, he eased away. For a moment she felt cool as he moved, then he draped the sheet over them and took her again in his arms, one hand stroking her thigh, hip, breast and back again. Lazy caresses, soothing at first but soon becoming exciting, building sensations that she'd thought had all been used up in their first cataclysmic mating.

Softly she said, 'I've always liked your hands.'

'You have?' He rested one on her hip, his thumb tracing the shape of the bone through the covering of flesh. 'I'm glad of that. Because my hands like you—like touching you. Especially here…and here, and here.' He found curves and hollows and planes, his clever fingers creating invisible flames that seemed to start under her skin and flicker over her, from her toes to her sweat-dewed temples. He kissed that away and then he kissed her cheek, her eyelids, her throat, before taking her sobbing breath in his mouth. She felt the intimate touch of his fingers and gave a small cry of pleasure.

Quinn lifted his mouth. 'I'm not hurting you?'

He stilled, ready to move away again, and she clutched his shoulders. 'No, it's wonderful. But I want *you*.'

She thought he smiled. 'You have me,' he said. 'Body, heart and soul.' He lowered his mouth once more to hers.

If only he meant it. She brushed away the intrusive, bitter little thought that men would say anything in the throes of lust. Maybe at this precise moment he did mean it. Maybe all thought of any other woman had been driven from his mind by the burning biological urge that possessed him.

His tongue parted her lips again, diving into her mouth, and she opened herself to him in every way, accepting his passion, his need, meeting it with her own in the sweet, tantalising duel of desire.

Everything faded from her mind but the urgent, overwhelming craving for release, mingling with the contradictory need to make this exquisite anticipation, so close to the summit of pleasure, last for ever.

Of course it didn't. They reached the peak almost together, his climax stimulated by her small, shuddering cries of fulfilment, and hers intensified and prolonged by the knowledge that he too was out of control, his whole body shaking in her arms.

They came down to the outer slopes of passion gradually, still locked together.

Then he moved and she reluctantly let him go, and he turned away, then padded off to the bathroom.

When he came back she was lying under the sheet, utterly relaxed and satisfied. He slipped an arm beneath her shoulders and she snuggled close. 'No regrets?' he said in a low voice.

'No.' She put a hand on his chest, liking the feel of him. 'You don't regret it, do you?'

His laughter shook his chest under her palm. 'Not a bit. I told you, I've wanted you for ages. It's been sheer torture living in this house with you, trying not to touch you. And it was my own stupid fault, making promises I couldn't keep.'

'You didn't do too badly. When did you…prepare for this?'

He stirred. 'After you told me that keeping to our agreement was hard for you too. I could stand it so long as I thought it was only me. I knew then that if you ever invited me to break the contract it would be hell to resist. A man can only take so much, and in case I weakened…'

'I'm glad you did.' She kissed his shoulder. Then yawned.

'Tired?'

'It's a nice tiredness. I haven't felt so relaxed in months.'

'D'you mind if I keep holding you while you go to sleep?'

'I'd like that.' She nuzzled her cheek against him and curled herself into his body, closing her eyes.

* * *

When she opened them again hours later light was streaming into the room. She lay on her back, and Quinn was propped on one elbow, watching her. They weren't touching any more, but they were only inches apart, with acres of bed on either side of them.

'I thought about waking you up,' Quinn said. 'But I wasn't sure how you'd react. We have a lot to learn about each other.'

'We've already learned a lot from living together for months.'

'There's heaps more I want to know about you.' He reached out and traced the line of her lips with one finger. 'Your mouth looks...swollen. Was that me?' He took his hand away.

'Guess so.' She experimentally ran her tongue over her lips. 'I'm not sore.'

'Not anywhere?'

'No.'

He shifted, coming closer so that his body touched hers, hip to hip. His hand found her waist, stroked up over her ribcage to her breast. 'Would you mind a repeat of last night?'

'No.' His hand felt good there, lightly touching her.

He smiled down at her. 'Are you always this talkative when you first wake?'

She raised her arms and hung them loosely about his neck. 'Who wants to talk?'

Quinn laughed. And then he kissed her.

It was different from the previous night, but just as satisfying. His lips, his hands went everywhere, and this time there was no hiding from the glitter of desire in his eyes when he flung back the sheet to look at her.

But Stefanie knew the same feverish sheen was in

her eyes as she looked back at him, boldly and without fear. He was magnificent, and when she took him into her again his arms wrapped her close until she was panting and twisting beneath him, and then he rolled over onto his back, giving her freedom to move and enjoy the pleasure to the full. She lay against him, spent, before he flipped them over again and drove to his own equally overwhelming climax.

'We're so good together,' he told her, lying quietly again beside her, holding her hand. He lifted it to his lips and nuzzled a kiss into her palm. 'Why have we wasted all this time?'

'Maybe it's better for the waiting,' she hazarded. 'Isn't it worth it?'

'Definitely it's worth it.' He leaned over and kissed her nose, his hand lingering on the curve of her waist. 'But I guess we should get up.'

'Yes.' Outside the world waited, and today it would be brighter.

CHAPTER TEN

STEFANIE always thought of the following weeks as her honeymoon. She went to work, and so did Quinn, and when she came home she'd wait for him and they'd swim together, playing about in the pool and teasing each other with fleeting touches, knowing it was really foreplay.

At dinner she sometimes found herself with a forgotten plate of half-finished food in front of her, because they'd been talking and she'd stopped eating.

They both still worked at night quite often, but Quinn's light no longer burned until after midnight, drawing ghostly flying insects into the yellow glow that played over the bushes outside the bedrooms.

While Stefanie bent over the dining table, making notes on cards, he would enter the room quietly and slide his arms about her, drop a kiss on her neck and whisper, 'Do you have to finish that, or can we go to bed?'

Most times she'd turn in his arms and tell him she didn't have to finish tonight. And they would end up in bed together, embarking on another phase in their journey of discovery of each other.

On Saturdays, instead of the popular beaches where half the island's population swam and snorkelled, canoed and fished, they sought out tiny secluded bays reached only by scrambling through untracked bush, or unpopulated areas of the highlands. They now habitually shared the same scooter, Stefanie riding pillion with her arms around Quinn's waist, her cheek pressed against his shoulder. They would leave the scooter at the roadside and trek to some shady, cool spot among the trees where no one would discover them. Lying on the rug that Quinn spread for them, they would read or sleep, or make love hidden by pink-leaved bushes, a canopy of banana leaves moving against the dazzling sky above them.

Several times they visited the waterfall again, and Stefanie remembered how Quinn had comforted her in her outpouring of grief, and then kissed her with unexpected passion. They kissed there again, standing in the water, and dried off afterwards on the mossy ground. But it was a fairly public spot, and sometimes other people would arrive without warning. They had to be circumspect to avoid shocking the locals.

On Sundays they visited nearby friends, but when Quinn looked over at her and fractionally lifted an eyebrow, his eyes sending a silent message, Stefanie would flush and make excuses and farewells, and they'd go home with their hands entwined, and fall into each other's arms almost as soon as they were in the door.

While Stefanie and Tom worked on the documents and books in the palace archives a team of carpenters added new shelves to the attic room for efficient storage and insulated the ceiling for coolness. Everything had been entered in the computer and backed up in case of disaster, and Stefanie and Tom began putting the folders and boxes and books onto the shelves in the right order. She was confident he would continue to keep the records up to date.

Quinn's project was up and running and Prince Tui

had found an expatriate Busiatan to take over the administrative work that Quinn had set up. 'Nearly time to go home, Stefanie,' Quinn said.

The thought inexplicably depressed her. 'Yes.' She couldn't say any more.

'We'll go to my apartment when we get to New Zealand, okay?' he asked her, quite casually. 'I hope you'll like it.'

'I'm sure I will.' A real marriage, he'd said. That meant a permanent one, didn't it? So why did she have this irrational fear that when they left Busiata everything would change?

The king gave them a farewell party, and Stefanie was surprised and touched at the number of people who came, and the overwhelming number of gifts that were pressed upon them.

The following day they boarded the plane for the journey to New Zealand.

When they landed in Auckland it was early morning. The air was cool and the sky grey. A taxi took them to Quinn's apartment on the fifth floor of a tall building.

The distant hum of traffic rose to the windows and the skyline was obscured by towers of concrete and glass. Between two of the adjacent buildings Stefanie caught a narrow glimpse of ships in the harbour.

The rooms were small and the furniture, Quinn said when she asked him, had come with the place. It was comfortable but bland, predominantly fawn and brown. After the bright, bold patterns favoured by the Busiatans, it looked drab and colourless.

'It's a bit different from Busiata.' Quinn slipped

his arms about her waist, his lips finding the indentation just below her ear.

She put her hands over his and leaned back against him. 'I'll miss it.' The warm tropical nights, the lazy clacking of the palm trees; the white sands and most of all the people, friendly and unhurried, always with time for a chat or a joke. She stirred. 'I'd better start unpacking, and then I'll phone my parents and let them know we're home.'

In the bedroom she paused before opening the suitcase that Quinn had placed at the foot of the bed. The coverlet was patterned in a jagged fawn and black design, with touches of metallic gold. The bed wasn't as big as the one they'd shared in his room at Busiata, but plenty big enough for two.

A fleeting picture of Quinn and Noelle, naked and entwined, flashed into her mind. She shook her head to banish it. No point in being oversensitive about the past. She was Quinn's wife now, in every sense, and if Noelle had once shared his bed that was all over. There was no going back—not for any of them.

She had brought home the wall hanging that she'd bought on the island. She would hang it in here, to remind her and Quinn of the coral beaches and blue waters of Busiata, of the warm tropical nights they had shared, and the hours they'd spent in each other's arms in secluded spots around the island. She would make this place as much theirs as their temporary tropical home had been, where they had first made love and become truly married.

But that night for the first time she found herself stiff and cold in Quinn's arms, trying to respond to his lovemaking but failing miserably.

'What is it?' he said at last, his hands stilling. 'What's the matter?'

'It's been a long day.' She tried to tell herself that was all it was.

'Why didn't you just tell me you weren't in the mood?'

'I didn't know until now. I'm sorry, Quinn.'

'It's okay.' He kissed her forehead. 'Go to sleep.'

But it was a long time before she was able to sleep.

Patti had extracted a promise that Stefanie would bring Quinn to see her parents. And Quinn admitted that his mother too had pressed for a visit. 'We might as well get them over with,' he said the next day. 'We can see our families this week, and then we'll settle ourselves in and I'll start hunting for an office and hiring staff.'

'And I can look for a job.'

He looked at her thoughtfully. 'How would you feel about working for me?'

'For you?'

'I told you I intend to employ staff. Your organisational and research skills would be very useful. There's a vast amount of information available on the internet, but it isn't always easy for people to find what they want.'

'There are lots of search engines on the internet that index what's available.'

'Too many of them are either confusing to use or rather limited. It's something I'd quite like to work on, and you're an expert on indexing and cross-referencing. If you're interested, I'll pay you a salary, of course.'

'It does sound interesting.' And the prospect of

working alongside Quinn, being with him every day, was alluring.

When they arrived at the Varney home, Patti opened the door as they were walking up the path, Quinn's arm about Stefanie's shoulders.

Patti flew down the steps and hugged her daughter. 'Are you all right, darling? You look wonderful!' Surprise etched her voice. She turned her gaze to Quinn. 'It was such a shock when she told us you were *married*!'

'I'm sorry about that,' he said calmly. 'But I was about to leave the country, you see, and I couldn't bear to go without her.' He smiled warmly down at Stefanie, who smiled gratefully back, silently thanking him for saving her pride. Why they'd really got married could remain a secret for ever now.

Patti looked suspiciously from one to the other of them, and seemed to relax. 'Well, come into the house. We're all here.'

Tracey came running down the steps, squealing her delight at her older sister's return, and Stephen Varney met them in the doorway, giving Stefanie a searching glance before he kissed her cheek and shook Quinn's hand. Gwenda and her husband were there too. 'Mind the bulge,' she warned as Stefanie went to hug her. 'This damned baby is already overdue and I'm as big as a house.'

'You look great,' Stefanie assured her. 'Pregnancy suits you.'

They had a leisurely family lunch, and when the dishes were disposed of Stefanie and Quinn showed everyone photographs of Busiata and handed out presents—a carved desk set for her father, some appliquéd bed.linen for her mother, sarongs for her two sisters and a shirt for Gwenda's husband. Handing over an exquisite appliquéd cot cover and an island-style baby's rattle to Gwenda, Stefanie saw a startled expression cross her sister's face and her hand go to her rounded belly.

'Gwenda? Are you all right?'

'Just a bit of indigestion, I think. I've been having it off and on since lunch.'

But a little later it became obvious that Gwenda was going into labour.

'He was just waiting for his aunty Stef to come home,' she joked as her chalk-faced husband held her hand and the rest of the family gathered about her. 'I suppose we'd better start thinking about going to the hospital.' She clutched at her stomach again as another contraction began. 'Zane,' she said to her husband, 'you'd better phone them and let them know we're on our way.'

'Good idea.' Zane jumped up immediately, gave his wife a clumsy kiss and a pat on the shoulder, and hurried out of the room.

Patti looked worried, her hands twisting together. 'Have you got a bag? Should someone fetch it?'

'In the car.' Gwenda gasped. 'I brought it along just in case this happened.'

Patti reached out to touch her arm. 'Poor darling. Is it bad? Shall I get you a cup of tea?'

'Thanks. That…would be nice. Tracey, why don't you help her?'

Tracey gave her sister a scared look and thankfully went after her mother.

When they'd both gone Gwenda took Stefanie's hand in hers. 'Stef,' she said, 'can you come to the hospital with me? The way Zane looks, I think he might be one of those husbands who faint, and Mum said she'd be there but you know how she is...'

Gwenda, the capable one of the family, wasn't feeling so capable now. 'I'd love to,' Stefanie said immediately. She turned to Quinn, and he nodded. 'Of course I'll come.' They were expecting to stay the night anyway.

Zane arrived back, clutching Gwenda's bag and looking anxious. 'What if we don't make it?' he blurted out. 'It's an hour's drive to the hospital.'

'You've done the classes with me,' Gwenda reminded him. 'You'll cope if you have to, Zane.'

'I'll drive you,' Quinn suggested. 'So you can concentrate on helping your wife.'

'And I'll come too,' Stefanie added firmly, interpreting Gwenda's silent plea for support. 'We'd better take some clean towels along just in case.'

Patti turned to her husband. 'Stephen...'

'We'll follow in our car,' he promised.

The towels weren't needed after all, because in the end the baby wasn't born until an hour after they had reached the hospital, with Zane, Patti and Stefanie in the birthing room while the others sat in the corridor.

Both her husband and her mother had surprised Gwenda by being remarkably calm and supportive. Only when it was all over, the baby wrapped in a blanket and placed in its mother's arms, Patti and Zane both became tearful, making Gwenda laugh. 'Here, take him,' she said to Stefanie, and the nurse standing nearby nodded, helping to transfer the tiny bundle from mother to aunt, and while Gwenda and her husband hugged each other Patti gratefully accepted a tissue from the nurse to wipe her eyes.

Stefanie was still holding her new nephew when the rest of the family was allowed in to meet him. She was gazing enraptured into his plump face and sleepy, fathomless eyes, and didn't look up until her father and sister came to admire him.

Then she raised her eyes and they met Quinn's grave stare, and she smiled.

Something quivered in his face, and she saw him swallow, his gaze going to the baby in her arms, before she turned to hand it back to its mother. While the others gathered about the bed she stepped back and felt Quinn's arm close about her. 'How was it?' he asked her in a low voice.

'Tough but worth it. I know Gwenda thinks so. Look at her.'

Her sister's face was aglow, her eyes lit with love as she looked from her husband to her baby.

Quinn's hand tightened on Stefanie's shoulder. He kissed her temple. 'She's certainly happy, and her husband's a different man.'

He was, flushed and proud. Stefanie laughed quietly. 'Gwenda was afraid he might faint, but he was great. He helped her a lot.'

Quinn would cope equally well, she thought. She couldn't imagine him fainting. He'd be good to have around at a birth—calm and competent and very protective. A piercing sense of longing assailed her. She wanted Quinn's child—children. Did he want to have children with her?

Stefanie and Quinn called again at the hospital the next morning, and then travelled further south to see his parents.

His father was a tall, grey-haired man and his

mother was small and rounded. Stefanie noticed the wedding photograph on top of the piano in the sitting room, where a much younger Mrs Branson looked rather like Noelle…

Both of them were polite and perhaps a bit wary at first, obviously as puzzled by their son's hasty marriage as Stefanie's parents had been. Wine was served with dinner, and maybe that eased the atmosphere. Afterwards the men walked around the flowerbeds that supplied the seed business, and Quinn's mother brought out a family photo album for Stefanie.

There were pictures of Quinn as a smiling, dark-haired boy growing from toddlerhood to near-teenage. In some of them he had his arm around a younger girl, thin and with hollowed eyes and a halo of fair hair.

'Janey, Quinn's little sister,' his mother said unsteadily. 'I suppose he's told you—she died.'

'Yes,' Stefanie said. 'I'm so sorry.' She was shocked to discover that her impression that Quinn hardly remembered his sister must have been quite wrong. And they had obviously been close.

'Yes. Quinn was awfully good with her—he looked after her from the time she was born. He was only three but he understood she needed special care. There was something wrong with her heart, you see, from birth. Now I believe there's an operation they can do, but she didn't live long enough for that.'

'That's terribly sad.' Stefanie felt the inadequacy of her response, but it was difficult to know what to say.

'I was afraid of sending her to school, but she wanted to be like other children, and Quinn looked out for her. When he was only nine he came home from school one day bleeding and dirty and looking terribly fierce, but he wouldn't say what had happened. Janey told us, though. Some children had been teasing her and he waded into them with his fists. He wouldn't let anyone hurt his sister.'

Mrs Branson sighed and shook her head. 'After she died he just closed right up for such a long time. He was just at the age where it's embarrassing for a boy to cry. Sometimes I think he's still bottling it up.' She turned another page and said with an effort at brightness, 'Quinn mentioned you have sisters.'

'Yes, there are three of us, all girls. I'm the eldest, but my next sister just had her first baby while Quinn and I were with my parents.'

'Oh, that's nice. Quinn should have a family. He'll make a good father. You're not...?'

'I'm not pregnant, no.' Quinn had made sure of that.

'Oh, I shouldn't ask.' Mrs Branson flushed. Maybe she'd thought that was why Quinn had married Stefanie so hurriedly—that he'd slept with her on the rebound and felt obliged to.

'You're his mother—you're entitled to ask.'

'Thank you, dear.' Mrs Branson patted her hand and closed the album. 'I always thought he needed a wife he could care for as he did Janey...someone to soften him again. That's why I thought maybe little Noelle was...'

'Right for him?' Stefanie guessed.

'Oh, dear.' Mrs Branson looked dismayed and embarrassed. 'I don't want to upset you!'

'It's all right. I'm not upset,' Stefanie assured her.

Quinn's mother looked relieved. 'You seem a nice, understanding sort of girl. After we lost Janey, all of a sudden Quinn seemed to be an adult, and I couldn't reach him any more.'

She must have felt she'd lost both her children.

Two days later they were back in Ratanui, drawing up outside Gwenda and Zane's house. As she usually did, Stefanie knocked briefly on the door before opening it and going straight in.

Hearing voices in the kitchen, she led Quinn through to the rear of the house, and came up short in the doorway.

Gwenda, the new baby in her arms, was seated at the round table with Zane beside her. Among the four cups on the table, a blue teddy bear with a ribbon about its neck lay in a nest of gift wrapping.

And opposite Gwenda and Zane sat Bryan and Noelle.

CHAPTER ELEVEN

For a moment no one moved or spoke. Gwenda's face showed her total horror, and Bryan flushed.

Then Zane jumped up. 'Hi!' he said much too heartily. 'You're back, then, you two! Um…Noelle and Bryan brought along a present for Junior.'

It was the sort of thing Noelle did automatically for anyone she knew—what everyone in Ratanui did when a friend or neighbour brought home a new baby. And Noelle had known Gwenda for as long as she had Stefanie. Stefanie shouldn't have been surprised to find her here, but why did it have to be today?

'We're just having coffee,' Zane said. 'Want some?'

Stefanie didn't, but she let Quinn answer yes for both of them and took the chair Zane had vacated when he offered it, with Quinn sitting between her and Noelle. Stefanie watched him turn to his ex-fiancée.

'How are you, Noelle?' he asked.

She blinked her violet eyes at him. 'Fine, thank you.' Taking her apprehensive gaze away from him, she let it skitter towards Stefanie, focusing somewhere near her left shoulder before meeting her erstwhile friend's eyes with a pleading look. 'How are you, Stefanie?'

'Very happy,' Stefanie replied. 'As I'm sure you are.'

Noelle gave a nervous giggle and said breathlessly,

'We were just telling Zane and Gwenda, we're going to have a baby too.'

Stefanie examined her feelings and decided that there was nothing there. 'That's nice.' Steeling herself, she looked at Bryan. Still nothing. Except, now, a sort of relief. She smiled, finding it suddenly easy. 'Congratulations, Bryan. You must be quite excited.'

He seemed taken aback. 'Yes. Thanks.' He jiggled his coffee cup, then lifted and emptied it.

'Not for a while yet, of course,' Noelle said. 'I'm not even three months on.'

Stefanie supposed that Noelle wanted them to know she hadn't been pregnant when she'd run off with Bryan. Well, that was pretty obvious. Her figure was only a tad more rounded than before, making her even more lush and adorable. The delicate flush on her cheeks made her as pretty as a chocolate-box picture, with a heart-catching air of quivering sensitivity, and Stefanie couldn't help being aware that Quinn had scarcely taken his eyes from his ex-fiancée since they'd walked in. Even without looking at him she sensed the direction of his hard stare. And he hadn't spoken to Bryan at all.

Perhaps Bryan noticed too. He cleared his throat and said, 'I hear you two have just come back from Busiata. Some big project or other, Quinn?'

Quinn didn't answer immediately, and Stefanie turned to him, wondering if he'd heard.

He wrenched his attention from Noelle and switched it to her husband, his eyes holding such hostility that Stefanie felt herself recoil, and Bryan jerked slightly in his chair. 'Yes,' Quinn said. He lifted an arm to lay it along the back of Stefanie's chair. 'It's a beautiful place and we had a great time, didn't we, darling?'

It was an instant before she realised he was addressing her. The only time he'd called her that was at the palace dinner when they'd first arrived on Busiata. But he was looking at her now, his eyes lit with some fierce, urgent message that she interpreted as, Play up to me, damn you!

Switching on a smile, she agreed, 'Yes, a wonderful time. It's a perfect place for...for a honeymoon.'

Noelle was looking from her to Quinn, a tiny frown between her carefully shaped brows, her cupid's-bow mouth almost pouting. 'But isn't it very hot there? And primitive?'

'Primitive—not at all. But very hot,' Quinn agreed smoothly. 'That's how we like it—hot.' He looked down again at Stefanie and his mouth curved into an intimate grin as he murmured, 'Don't we?'

Stefanie very nearly laughed at Noelle's almost indignant expression. But she was also angry at Quinn for using her to score off the other woman. She dropped a hand to his thigh, making it look like a caress, and giving him a painful little pinch.

She felt his reaction, heard the quick intake of breath, though his face gave nothing away.

Bryan cleared his throat again. 'Well, we'll be on our way. Are you going to finish that coffee, Noelle?'

'I've had enough.' She scrambled up hastily, apparently just as eager to leave as he was. 'Thanks, Gwenda, and Zane. I hope our baby's as cute as yours when it's born.' She flashed them a false smile, then skimmed it over Quinn and Stefanie. 'It was nice seeing you two again.'

Stefanie nodded, quite unable to return the conventional lie, and made an effort to smile back. Quinn watched Zane usher them out, and as they disappeared along the passageway Gwenda said in an anguished whisper, 'I'm so sorry! I was hoping like hell they'd be gone before you arrived.'

Stefanie picked up her untouched coffee. 'We were bound to run into each other eventually. Don't worry about it.'

'I've only been civil to them,' Gwenda said. 'I don't believe in carrying on feuds. It was decent of them to bring the baby a present, though. Makes me feel a bit awful. I think Noelle's lonely, because none of our friends want anything to do with her and Bryan.'

Zane came back, letting out a whistle. 'Sorry about that.'

'No problem,' Quinn assured him evenly. 'We have a present too. Stefanie?' His gaze flickered to her, not quite meeting her eyes.

She'd been holding the parcel on her lap—so tightly, she now realised, that its jaunty blue bow was creased and flattened.

'Another one?' Gwenda exclaimed. 'You've already given us presents for him.'

'We couldn't resist this.' She and Quinn had spotted the ferocious-looking, fat stuffed cat with uneven button eyes and one bent ear in a shop window on their journey north, and when they'd stopped laughing she had promptly bought it, despite his warning her that it would terrify her poor nephew.

She handed the package over, trying not to notice that when Quinn forgot to smile his jaw was so tightly clenched she could see the rigidity of the muscles. And that he never looked at her.

*   *   *

Two hours later they were on their way back to Auckland. Quinn sat in grim silence, and every so often the needle on the dashboard crept well over the speed limit, until he apparently noticed and reduced the pressure of his foot on the accelerator.

Tongue-tied and despondent, Stefanie watched the green farms and small towns and rows of telephone lines flash by, and tried to tell herself that Quinn wasn't eaten up with regrets.

They were gliding up a steep rise when another car passed them and had to cut in rather too quickly as a milk tanker loomed over the brow of the hill.

Quinn braked and let fly an expletive Stefanie had never heard him use before. 'Bloody fool!' he added savagely.

Tacitly Stefanie agreed, but she'd never known Quinn to be obviously bad-tempered before—except after Noelle had run off with Bryan, and he'd come down from Auckland, demanding to know if Stefanie knew where his fiancée was, and told her frankly that he was bloody furious.

And now, although as usual he was reining in his temper, he was rather obviously in a quiet, towering rage.

Stefanie bit her lip. Of course none of them had been exactly overwhelmed with joy to see each other today, and without any warning. Bryan had been acutely uncomfortable, Stefanie herself tongue-tied with embarrassment, and Noelle's bright smiles totally failed to hide the fact that she was wishing herself somewhere else.

Quinn and Stefanie's arrival had spoiled Noelle's pleasure in telling Zane and Gwenda her exciting news. Poor Noelle. Despite the core of anger that still surfaced sometimes, Stefanie found it hard to hate her. She'd looked so scared when Quinn sat down beside her, and her eyes when she'd forced them to meet Stefanie's had been apologetic and miserable.

Noelle had never been brave. And it wasn't only men who felt she needed protection. Even Gwenda was sorry for her because now she had no friends in her home town.

All through their childhood and right up until the stunning betrayal that tore them apart Stefanie had been Noelle's friend, confidante, champion. But Stefanie couldn't help her now. They could never, surely, be truly friends again. She swallowed on a hard lump in her throat, trying not to feel the hurt of that.

Tears shimmered in her eyes. She tried to blink them away but one slid down her cheek, and she turned to the side window, the view of green paddocks and tranquilly grazing cows blurring as she surreptitiously wiped her eyes with her fingers.

It didn't help, and she had to fumble for her bag on the floor and find a tissue. Quinn glanced at her, said something under his breath and flattened the accelerator to the floor, passing a green sheep truck with a roar before slackening speed again. By the time she had dealt with her emotions and dared to look at him again his expression was grimmer than ever, his mouth clamped in a harsh line, his hands fists about the steering wheel.

The journey seemed interminable, but at last he garaged the car and hauled their luggage out of the boot, curtly refusing Stefanie's offer to help.

He took the bags into the bedroom and she followed, but as soon as he'd dumped the luggage on the carpet he went straight into the bathroom and she heard the shower running.

Stefanie put away her shoulder bag, then slipped off her jacket and hung it in the wardrobe. Closing the mirrored door, she caught sight of herself, her face pale but her cheekbones flushed, and her eyes slightly pink. Damn.

Hurrying to the kitchen, she splashed cold water over her eyes, then dabbed at them with a towel and took two deep breaths before returning to the bedroom.

She went in and found Quinn had finished showering and was standing by his chest of drawers, a towel loosely fastened about his hips as he threw a few items of clothing onto the bed.

He slammed the drawer shut and turned, stopping dead as he saw her. 'I thought you were in the kitchen.' His gaze was almost accusing, his eyes narrowing on her face, and she knew the cold water she'd used on her eyes hadn't done much good.

'Only for a minute.' She took a step towards the little huddle of bags, with some vague idea of starting to unpack.

His abrupt movement made her look at him again. He strode to the bed, tugging impatiently at his towel and throwing it on the floor.

Stefanie paused, both wary and fascinated. She'd seen him naked before, male and potent and sexy, but he'd never deliberately flaunted himself like this, challenging her to react.

Reaching out, he grabbed a pair of underpants off the bed and straightened with them in his hand, his dark gaze going to her face. 'Enjoying yourself?' he jeered.

He was still angry. And he was aroused. The shower, she guessed, had been a cold one, but it hadn't helped a lot more than her dousing of her reddened eyes had.

She wasn't all that pleased with him either. All the time they'd sat, tortured and grimly civilised, at her sister's table, Stefanie might not have existed for him any more. He'd asked her to make their marriage real, but the very first time he'd laid eyes on Noelle again he'd scarcely been able to tear them away from her. So which woman had caused this unmistakable physical arousal?

Jealousy coursed through her in a hot, evil tide, like nothing she'd ever known. Her cheekbones burned and her chest felt as if her heart would burst through it. Tilting her chin, she said, 'Obviously *you're* ready to enjoy yourself.'

His hand closed on the garment he held. '*Don't* goad me, Stefanie!' he warned, his eyes glittering. 'You might get more than you bargained for.'

She knew how he felt, because she felt exactly the same; a violent, volatile, dangerous mix of emotions—rage, despair, hurt and desire. And if his desire was really for Noelle—only diverted to Stefanie because she was here and Noelle wasn't—well, at least he'd called her by her own name. She *wasn't* Noelle and they both knew it.

And this might be her last card.

Recklessly she looked back at him, unflinching defiance in her eyes. 'Well,' she said, in a husky, deliberately provocative voice, 'so might you.'

For just an instant his face reflected shocked disbelief. Then he said gratingly, 'Sorry. I'm not in the mood.'

Stefanie laughed. It was such a patent lie. And she needed some kind of release from the unbearable tension that shimmered tangibly in the air.

It snapped him. He flung the underpants after the discarded towel, strode over to her and hauled her into his naked arms, covering her mouth with his and smothering the laughter in a kiss that had no preliminary and no gentleness.

A kiss to which she responded in kind, the dark flame within her leaping to meet the primitive fire of passion in him. She arched against him, her hands sliding to his hips, then up over his ribs as he drove the kiss deeper, hotter, until her ears hummed and she was breathing fast into his mouth.

His hands thrust into her hair and he dragged his mouth to her throat, pressed a kiss on her shoulder, then nipped the tender skin of her breast with his teeth so that for an instant she felt a faint thrill of fear, but the sensation was wholly pleasurable.

Quinn was shaking, and so was she.

His head jerked up and his eyes blazed at hers. 'You should stop me,' he said, his voice guttural, almost inaudible through his clenched teeth.

'Can't you stop yourself?' she taunted him, her eyes wide and bright.

'Damn you, no!' His hand still in her hair, tightly clutching a fistful of it, he kissed her again, as devastatingly as before. And then he lifted her and practically tossed her onto the bed, trapping her there with his legs as he tore every scrap of clothing from her. She heard stitches rip and felt elastic give way, and didn't care. Neither did he. She knew he was beyond caring about anything but a driving need to bury his body in hers. She could see it in his tightly clenched, unsmiling face and ferally glittering eyes.

Poised over her, he muttered, 'You asked for this.'

Fearlessly she stared back at him, her eyes hot and open. 'So when are you going to give it to me?'

'*Stefanie!*' The cry seemed wrenched from deep inside him, desperate and anguished.

Every muscle taut and strained as piano wire, he hesitated for an age, his face sheened with sweat and his eyes half closed.

Stefanie couldn't bear it. She moved her hips invitingly, found him with her hand to guide him. And he gave a great moan and sank into her, onto her, wrapped his arms about her and began to move inside her.

Only seconds later they plunged into the golden fire together, consumed in each other for endless time, wave after wave of incandescent heat racking them until the last echoing shudders gradually, inevitably subsided.

Stefanie lay exhausted, her eyes closed, her whole being in a state of complete lethargy.

And for the first time ever Quinn immediately removed himself from her, his arms falling away as he rolled over to lie on his back. When she tiredly peeked, hardly able to lift her heavy lids, he was lying utterly still, his forearm flung over his eyes.

She must have fallen asleep within minutes. When she woke it was fully daylight and Quinn wasn't there.

Stifling unease, she had a shower and made the bed. Dressed in jeans and a shirt, trying to appear nonchalant, she went in search of her husband.

Quinn was in the kitchen, an empty coffee cup in

front of him. He'd been staring into space, but when she appeared in the doorway he looked up, his eyes so devoid of any emotion they appeared strangely opaque. He had a suit on. A tie. He looked devastatingly handsome, and just the sight of him made her heart squeeze tight.

'Hello,' she said. She had difficulty getting the word past her throat. Her voice sounded husky.

'Good morning.'

'Are you going out?' she asked.

The newspaper was folded in front of him. He looked down at it as if he'd forgotten it was there. 'There's an office space advertised that seems promising. I thought I should look at it.'

'I see.' There was an inch of coffee left in the percolator. Quinn couldn't be on his first cup—they always filled the jug to halfway. Stefanie went over and emptied it into a mug, switched off the machine and went back to the table.

About to sit down, she paused, staring at the small oblong of paper lying on the wooden surface. A cheque.

She saw the name of Quinn's bank, and her name in his handwriting with decisive downstrokes and bold, rounded loops.

Her temples went cold, and her hands closed clammily about the coffee mug. 'What's that?'

'Your payment under our agreement.'

Stefanie put the mug down on the table in case she dropped it. Hot coffee splashed over her hand but she scarcely noticed. 'I don't want it. Things have changed.'

'One part of the agreement has been well and truly broken, I agree—by mutual consent. But we had a contract and you more than fulfilled your part. The money's yours—you earned it. Do what you like with it.'

What she would like to do was to tear up the cheque and throw the pieces in his face.

She reached out to pick it up and do just that, but his voice stopped her. She still hadn't sat down, and he stood up to face her, his hands curled over the back of his chair, the knuckles white. His face was pale too. He looked as if he was feeling sick.

'I'm truly sorry about last night, Stefanie. More than you'll ever know.'

'For God's sake!' she snapped. 'It was hardly rape!'

'It was worse than that.'

'Worse?'

'I seem to have made a habit of taking advantage of you when you're in no state to resist. Last night— what I did was unforgivable.'

Because he'd used her—substituted her for Noelle? Maybe he'd closed his eyes and pretended she *was* Noelle. And now he was racked with guilt.

'I knew what you were doing,' Stefanie said thinly. 'And you gave me the chance to stop you.' She could barely speak for pain, as if someone had driven a blunt knife into her throat. Of course she had known—or guessed—that his passion last night had been a displaced emotion, misdirected because Noelle wasn't available and she was. But hearing him practically admit it was more hurtful than she'd ever dreamed. 'I know you would have stopped,' she said, 'if I'd asked you to.'

'I can't understand why you didn't. It's all right, I'm not expecting you to explain. I guess you needed some kind of...catharsis. I hope it helped. But that doesn't excuse me for being totally selfish and manipulative. It wasn't a mistake that I didn't use anything. I did it on purpose...and I'm sorry. I can promise you it's the very first time for me, but I could have made you pregnant.'

The room seemed to tilt. That was what he was apologising for—feeling so guilty about? Not using a contraceptive? Deliberately? What did that mean?

'It's...unlikely,' she said, her head still swimming as she tried to concentrate on the point that was obviously worrying him. 'One time.'

'If you are—' his voice suddenly deepened '—I'll stand by you, to whatever degree you want. But that cheque gives you your freedom. What you do now—' he paused, and she saw him swallow '—is entirely your choice.'

'My choice?' She had chosen to be his wife in every sense of the word. And she'd hoped that meant permanence. For ever. Until death.

Did he want her to leave? Had seeing Noelle proved to him that this makeshift marriage was in truth the sham it had started out to be, that he could never love another woman—certainly not the woman he'd legally tied himself to?

Her hands clutched the chair in front of her, because the room seemed to be spinning and she needed to hang onto something. And she needed to *think*. Because something wasn't making sense. But she could feel her insides splintering into tiny, painful pieces, making logical thought impossible.

Why had she thought her heart was broken when Bryan left her? What she'd felt then was nothing compared with the way she was tearing apart inside now. Quinn had called her pragmatic because she hadn't become hysterical when Bryan jilted her. She simply hadn't known what real love was. How could anyone survive a rejection like this? Afraid of howling her anguish out loud, she clamped her teeth together and tried to breathe.

'Last night,' Quinn said, 'I'd have done anything to keep you, to make you stay with me and have my child...children. In the cold light of day I see how desperately wrong that was. I know I can't atone adequately for such appalling behaviour. You must decide if you can ever forgive me. And...if you want to leave...I can't blame you, but I don't want to be here to see it.'

He picked up the newspaper and folded it once more, frowning down at it and aligning the edges as though it was the most important thing in the world.

'What made you think I wouldn't have stayed anyway?' she asked him, dimly realising that she was missing something vital.

Reluctantly he looked at her. 'You cried. Yesterday, in the car after...'

Yesterday? What did yesterday have to do with anything? She wrenched her thoughts back. 'After we met Bryan and Noelle? Well, what about *you*?' Gaining a little confidence, she said it with fierce demand. She had the right.

'Me?'

'You hardly took your eyes off Noelle all the time they were there. And you looked about ready to kill Bryan if he so much as moved in a way you didn't like.'

'Of *course* I want to kill him! After what he did to you I've wanted to punch him to kingdom come, if you'd only let me. But there you were being nice to him, smiling at him, congratulating him on his baby. And I remembered how I felt when I saw you holding your sister's and realised I wanted to see you hold our baby, look at my child like that. I already knew I loved you...'

'What?'

He didn't seem to hear her strangled exclamation. 'At that moment I knew for sure that this was never going to go away, that it was quite different from what I'd felt for Noelle or for any other woman—stronger, deeper, truer. I love your courage, and your maturity, and your unexpected passion. Everything about you, every new thing I discover each day.'

Something bright seemed to burst behind her eyes. Oddly furious, she cried, 'Then *why* were you staring at Noelle like that?'

He seemed taken aback. 'Was I staring? I suppose I was. Trying to work out what I'd ever seen in her, to remember why I ever thought I was in love with her. She seemed like a stranger, not someone I'd ever been close to. All I could feel for her was a sort of weary pity and exasperation. I couldn't live with her. I never want to live with any woman but you.'

'She's like your sister,' Stefanie said.

'My sister?' He stared. 'Maybe you're right,' he conceded. 'Superficially. In a way I felt about her the way I used to about Janey. I suppose for a while Noelle filled that space that seemed to have been hollowed out in my heart ever since I was thirteen.'

'Has the hollow feeling come back again since Noelle ditched you?' she asked with some trepidation.

'Not until last night...when I realised what I'd done, making love to you like that.'

She waited for him to say more, because he seemed about to, but then he closed his lips tightly and said, 'I'll leave you to think things over.'

Stefanie guessed what he was doing. He'd told her he loved her, but hadn't asked for her response. Last night he'd acted totally out of character, and now he was determined not to resort to emotional blackmail. He wouldn't ask for her compassion, coerce her declaration of love.

'Quinn?'

He had reached the door, but his fingers stilled on the handle. His voice muffled, he said, 'Yes.'

'I wasn't crying over Bryan yesterday. I'd already done with all that. I never cared for him half as much as I do for you. I was crying for lost friendship, and because Noelle needs friends now and this time there's no way I can help her, but mostly...I was crying because I was afraid you were still in love with her, that I'd never have all of your heart. And I couldn't bear that, because I love you too much.'

He turned around very slowly. 'You love me?'

'You never said it to me before today,' she accused him.

'I thought you didn't want to hear it.' He looked dazed. 'That it was too soon. I only hoped that one day you would be ready. The first time we made love I couldn't help telling you my feelings...but you didn't give me any answer.'

You have me, he'd told her. *Body, heart and soul.*

'I didn't believe it,' she confessed. 'I thought that was passion speaking.'

He tossed aside the paper he still held and crossed the room swiftly to take her in his arms. 'Believe me,' he said, 'I absolutely adore you, and if you love me even half as much I'll be happy.'

'Twice as much,' she argued, her arms sliding about his neck. 'What on earth did you think last night was all about, for me? I was trying to make sure you couldn't leave me, to bind you to me with chains of gold.'

'Chains of gold?' His eyes gleamed. 'Sounds kinky.' But his voice was unsteady.

'It's a quotation, I think. I read it somewhere.'

'You don't need chains of any sort,' he said, and kissed her thoroughly, completely, with passion but underlying tenderness. Then he rubbed his cheek against her temple. 'You feel so right in my arms. You always did, from the time I first kissed you properly at the waterfall. I'm bound to you for ever, and chains of iron wouldn't make that any more so. I've offered you your freedom once, but it cost me, and I don't think I could ever do it again.'

'I am free,' she told him. 'Free to love you. That's our gift to each other—a never-ending gift we can share for all our lives.' She reached up and kissed his mouth, whispered, 'Are you still going out?'

'Hell, no! I'm taking you back to bed.'

She laughed at him. 'You need to find us an office.'

'I need *you*,' he argued, swinging her up into his arms and taking her to the bedroom. 'More than I'll ever need anything for the rest of my life. Later we'll go and have a look at the place—together. I may never go anywhere without you again.'

'That would be nice,' she murmured as he lowered her to the bed and lay beside her. 'I'd like to come with you.'

'I hope to arrange that very soon,' he promised, and smothered her laughter with his mouth as she flung her arms about him and joyously returned his kiss.

MILLS & BOON®

Makes any time special

Enjoy a romantic novel from
Mills & Boon®

Presents™ *Enchanted*™ *Temptation*®

Historical Romance™ *Medical Romance*™

MILLS & BOON®

Next Month's Romance Titles

♡

Each month you can choose from a wide variety of romance novels from Mills & Boon®. Below are the new titles to look out for next month from the Presents™ and Enchanted™ series.

Presents™

LOVER BY DECEPTION	Penny Jordan
THE SECRET MISTRESS	Emma Darcy
HAVING HIS BABIES	Lindsay Armstrong
ONE HUSBAND REQUIRED!	Sharon Kendrick
THE MARRIAGE QUEST	Helen Brooks
THE SEDUCTION BID	Amanda Browning
THE MILLIONAIRE'S CHILD	Susanne McCarthy
SHOTGUN WEDDING	Alexandra Sellers

Enchanted™

A NINE-TO-FIVE AFFAIR	Jessica Steele
LONE STAR BABY	Debbie Macomber
THE TYCOON'S BABY	Leigh Michaels
DATING HER BOSS	Liz Fielding
BRIDEGROOM ON LOAN	Emma Richmond
BABY WISHES AND BACHELOR KISSES	Valerie Parv
THERE GOES THE BRIDE	Renee Roszel
DADDY WOKE UP MARRIED	Julianna Morris

On sale from 4th June 1999

H1 9905

Available at most branches of WH Smith, Tesco, Asda, Martins, Borders, Easons, Volume One/James Thin and most good paperback bookshops

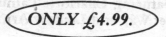

FREE!

4 Books
and a surprise gift!

We would like to take this opportunity to thank you for reading this Mills & Boon® book by offering you the chance to take FOUR more specially selected titles from the Presents™ series absolutely FREE! We're also making this offer to introduce you to the benefits of the Reader Service™ —

- ★ FREE home delivery
- ★ FREE gifts and competitions
- ★ FREE monthly Newsletter
- ★ Books available before they're in the shops
- ★ Exclusive Reader Service discounts

Accepting these FREE books and gift places you under no obligation to buy; you may cancel at any time, even after receiving your free shipment. Simply complete your details below and return the entire page to the address below. *You don't even need a stamp!*

YES! Please send me 4 free Presents books and a surprise gift. I understand that unless you hear from me, I will receive 6 superb new titles every month for just £2.40 each, postage and packing free. I am under no obligation to purchase any books and may cancel my subscription at any time. The free books and gift will be mine to keep in any case.

P9EB

Ms/Mrs/Miss/Mr ....Initials ....
BLOCK CAPITALS PLEASE

Surname..

Address..

....

....Postcode ....

Send this whole page to:
THE READER SERVICE, FREEPOST CN81, CROYDON, CR9 3WZ
(Eire readers please send coupon to: P.O. BOX 4546, DUBLIN 24.)

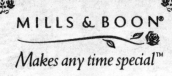